The Wedding was a Hollywood Dream . . .

Carey glanced up at Oliver. How different he was now! He was being friendly and charming to everyone. Or was he putting up a front to convince all these people this wedding was born in heaven and destined for a paradise on earth?

She wondered if he liked her in her wedding dress. She wondered what he thought about her at all.

She wondered what it would be like when he kissed her. For he had not kissed her yet . . .

Wife To Order

Lucy Walker

BEAGLE BOOKS • NEW YORK
An Intext Publisher

Published by arrangement with Crown Publishers, Inc.

First printing: June, 1971

Printed in the United States of America

BEAGLE BOOKS, INC.
101 Fifth Avenue, New York, NY 10003

CHAPTER ONE

Carey sat, her hands folded neatly in her lap, and looked across the distance of wide desk at the man Uncle Tam had brought her to see.

Oliver Reddin had shaken hands with her, smiled briefly, and called her Miss Fraser.

He was very tall, very good-looking, very well-groomed and had impeccable but distant manners. Carey felt that in straying into his presence she was wandering in strange lands. She had had the same feeling in coming to this great, rich, well-kept, industrious and beautiful station. Coming from a town outback of the grasslands, Carey had never before seen the tender green of willows along a creek bed: or the deep green of a pine plantation growing on the slopes of the hill along the bottom of which had run the road she and Uncle Tam had come by.

By Carey's standards this wasn't a homestead at all. It was a great lovely house, two storied and set about with wide gardens, standing dignified in an ocean of green grass.

When a housemaid, in conventional black dress and white lace-edged apron, had shown them into the wide hall, Carey had looked around, captivated and awed. It must have shown in her face because Uncle Tam had touched her arm and said:

"There, there, Carey!" in a soothing voice. "There's nothing to be worried about. Your father knew Mr. Reddin, and Mr. Reddin's father before him. He won't eat you. And he must have had something mighty good about him for your father to make him executor of your estate."

Carey couldn't get over this word "estate." She had always known her father had a property in Western Victoria and that there was a manager running it and taking a share of the profits. The profits had dwindled and dwindled disastrously. Her father had been too sick to make the effort to do anything about investigating the causes of the trouble way down in Western Victoria: and Uncle Tam had been too old.

Carey and her father had gone to live with Uncle Tam

outback ten years ago now. That was when her father had first been taken with his illness. Uncle Tam had given them a home because someone had to keep an eye on the eight-year-old girl while his brother Reg slowly gave up his slender hold on life.

She had been a young gay little girl with a round sweet face and smiling, happy ways. The people in the dusty little town out beyond the range and across the dust bowl had taken Carey to their hearts. She had grown up to the age of eighteen in the shelter of her uncle's ramshackle homestead and in the warm glow of everybody's love.

When she was sixteen people used sometimes to say Carey should go away to Sydney or Melbourne and learn some trade or profession.

" She'll be needing it," they used to say, shaking their heads. " What with poor Reg Fraser the way he is, and you're not so young, Tam . . ."

Uncle Tam would shake his head and say:

" She can't be leaving her father now. It wouldn't be human. Yes, I know I'm getting on, but Reg has got a bit of property down there in Western Victoria . . . and she won't be left with nothing. She'll still be young when he's gone and what with her pretty face and a bit of property she'll have time to learn something that'll help so as she'll look after herself."

When Carey's father died she was just eighteen years old. Her father's will had been very simple. It left everything to Carey and made Mr. Oliver Reddin of Two Creeks, Victoria, executor of the estate.

Uncle Tam had written to Mr. Reddin at once . . .

First they had had two days in Melbourne and Uncle Tam had taken Carey to Myers's big store in Bourke Street and said to a woman in the dress department:

" Fit her out, will you. And fix someone to buy her a nice hat like all the smart young ladies in Collins Street are wearing. Maybe she could have her hair cut . . . and all fixed up."

The woman, tall, grey-haired and kindly, had smiled at the little old outback man and the bewildered girl.

" You go away, Mr. Fraser," she had said gently. " Come back at about three o'clock this afternoon. We'll look after your niece."

" Well now, what about lunch . . ." began the old man.

" Don't you worry about lunch," said the kindly woman.

"Miss Fraser can have something light while she is having her hair set . . . or before she has her manicure."

"Manicure?" Uncle Tam asked, astounded.

"Of course. In Melbourne every young lady has her hands manicured."

Uncle Tam and Carey had exchanged a smile, and he had shrugged his shoulders.

"Well," he said, "I hadn't thought of it, I'll grant you. But if you think it necessary . . ."

Carey looked at the woman's long slender hands and the pink fingernails.

"I'd *like* it," she said, and there was real shining pleasure in her eyes.

"It's absolutely necessary," the woman said again. "When you smile like that, my dear, and when we've dressed you . . ."

She let her words trail away into nothing, but before Carey's inexperienced imaginative eyes there suddenly unrolled vistas of beauty and sophistication.

Uncle Tam didn't have very much money, but her father had left her an "estate." Uncle Tam had said not to worry about the cost of anything. Mr. Reddin of Two Creeks would fix it all up.

Now, in her new dress of royal blue silk that made her eyes a deeper blue and brought out the soft glow of her youthful face under the soft white small-brimmed hat, Carey sat with Uncle Tam in Mr. Reddin's study and looked at him.

In her own heart, when she stole sidelong glances at him, she had called him "terrific," even though he was a lot older than herself. He would be at least thirty. Probably more. He was the most handsome and well-dressed man she had ever seen. He had black hair and a straight nose and a very firm chin. He only smiled once . . . when they came in . . . and then she saw his teeth were white, even and strong. Ever since then his eyes, grey and clear, had been cold . . . She herself had been very quiet, and Uncle Tam wasn't arguing, which said a lot. Uncle Tam generally argued with everyone. Outback, Carey had spent a good deal of her time being nice and kind to people Uncle Tam had been arguing with, so they wouldn't be offended. Someone had once called her a regular little peace-maker, and one time their storekeeper had said:

"This town'll look after those two Fraser brothers long

as you're alive, young Carey. Real dose of sunshine, you are. And always pouring oil on troubled waters into the bargain."

Sitting beside Mr. Reddin's desk, his broad-brimmed felt hat on the floor beside him, his gnarled and ancient hands resting on the polished desk top, Uncle Tam was *not* arguing.

Mr. Reddin didn't know how lucky he was.

Presently Mr. Reddin got up, dug his hands in his pockets and walked round the desk. Then he walked round Carey, looking at her.

Carey's eyes followed him so that her head too went round as he went round. Then she lowered her eyes and looked at her hands in her lap.

Mr. Reddin went back to his chair. Suddenly he put his hands, palm down, firmly on the desk.

"Now, what's to be done?" he said.

Carey could see quite clearly that he *was* angry. Very angry in a cold controlled kind of way.

"You'll have to figure it out somehow, Oliver," Uncle Tam said with a mollifying voice that rang a danger bell for Carey. Uncle Tam was up to something.

"I can't give her a home any longer. 'Sides, it's no place for a young girl like Carey. Just take a look at her. She's kinda soft bred. And all elegant as if she's just come out of a finishing school. You couldn't ask her to go back, now she's a young lady, to a place like Wybong."

Carey's startled eyes met her uncle's, but rather sheepishly he looked away back to Mr. Reddin.

"You see what I mean," Uncle Tam was saying. "You're the executor, Mr. Reddin. There must be some way of saving that farm."

So this was why Uncle Tam had taken her to that huge store and had her dressed up, polished, manicured and shod; to pass her off on Mr. Reddin!

"Uncle Tam . . ." she said pleadingly.

He leaned over and patted her hand.

"There, there, Carey, don't you worry," he said. "Mr. Reddin here will give you a home until such times . . ."

"I'll do nothing of the kind," said Oliver Reddin flatly. His grey eyes were cold with anger. "You are Miss Fraser's only living relative. Her uncle, in fact."

"Now, now," said Uncle Tam with affected sadness. "She's eighteen and outside the law so far as any relative having

8

to keep her. I can't give her a home any more, Mr. Reddin. And it's not fair on the girl . . ."

"Miss Fraser," Mr. Reddin said quietly, "would you mind sitting on one of those chairs over by the wall? I think it is better that your uncle and I discuss this in private."

"Very well, Mr. Reddin," Carey said quietly. She got up and walked across the big room to a row of semi-armchairs under the window. Her heart was beating painfully fast. What should she do if Uncle Tam would not take her home and Mr. Reddin didn't want to bother finding some place for her to live?

She sat thinking, as the two men at the other end of the room went on talking. Her heart beat so fast it almost hurt and unconsciously she clasped her hands and held them pressed against her breast to quiet that rapid beating, but it was a peculiarly poignant gesture.

Mr. Reddin, at the other end of the room, saw it. He pulled in the corners of his mouth and his eyes became angry again. He turned back to Uncle Tam. Carey thought she knew why Mr. Reddin was cold with anger. Her father had made him her executor probably without consulting him, and now he found her, and her affairs, a packet of trouble on his hands. Carey was sorry, but more than her sorrow was her own anger that he should show it all so plainly.

The door, which had been closed when Carey and her uncle came in, began slowly and silently to open. First there was a crack and then there were the fingers of a small hand showing round the edge. Inch by inch the door opened wide enough to allow a small body to enter.

Fascinated, Carey watched a boy enter the room, shut the door stealthily behind him and then walk tiptoe across the room towards herself. He sat down in the chair beside her and when he eased himself back on the seat his feet no longer touched the ground. He would be about seven years old, Carey thought.

He looked up at her, and their eyes met.

His hands were clean and his face was shining. Between his fingers and along the hairline was a dampness that told her he had just washed himself but not dried himself very well. There had been some attempt to do his hair which was badly in need of cutting but at the back the hair round the crown of his head stood on end as if it had been many a day since it had seen brush or comb.

9

Whatever attempt he had made to clean himself up, it had not gone beyond his brown-eyed face, hands and the front part of his hair.

Before she could speak Mr. Reddin had turned in his chair and suddenly saw the pair sitting side by side, silent, under the window. He stood up with a sudden movement. "What the devil are you doing there?" he asked. He looked at the boy. "Where did you come from? Have you run away from that place again?"

He came round the table and across the room and stood towering over the boy.

"Tony! Answer me at once. How did you get here?"

"I walked, sir!"

"You walked! Twenty miles! How? Across the paddocks by the look of things. Clear out of here, do you hear me? And when I've finished I'll come outside and give you the kind of thrashing that will keep you walking for six months."

Tony slid off the chair and stood up. He did not appear to be afraid of Oliver Reddin but Carey fairly quailed at the anger in his voice.

Tony glanced sideways at Carey. He looked very odd standing there by the tall man, quite unafraid of the storm that was thundering over his head. Then he looked up at Mr. Reddin.

"Is she another orphan, too?" he asked.

"Certainly not." He stopped short on the words and suddenly looked at Carey intently. "At least, not exactly," he amended. He turned away towards Carey's uncle. "You see what I mean?" he said in exasperation. "I've enough trouble with that one on my hands . . ." With a nod of his head he indicated Tony.

There was a tap at the door and the housemaid came in.

"Excuse me, Mr. Oliver . . ." she began, and then saw Tony. "Oh, there you are!" She looked back at Oliver Reddin. "Cook told me she saw him sidling in by the west veranda. Then I found the mess in the bathroom. Sir . . . please . . . what are we to do with him?"

"Take him out and drown him," Oliver Reddin said with exasperation. Then as he went back to the desk, he added, "For heaven's sake clean him up and feed him first."

He sat down and ran his fingers through his hair.

"Look, Mr. Fraser . . ." his voice came across the room

to Carey, " that farm is valuable land. I've watched it running down and the bracken and blackberry and paspalum creeping back on the road paddocks. The out-paddock is almost back to bush again. Legally, I can sell it, wind up the estate and be shot of the whole business. But as executor I'm honour bound to make the best deal for her. That means jacking up that farm. It's next door to me. It can be done. I'm asking myself how much trouble and expense it is going to be, and you tell me she hasn't got a home. Meantime you're in there at the Junee Hotel running up God knows what kind of an expense account."

Carey turned her head and looked out the window and then back at her hands.

Did Uncle Tam really mean he wouldn't give her a home any more? Or was he playing one of those cunning tricks that always got him into so much trouble at home?

" Mr. Reddin . . ." she said in her quiet gentle voice. " I could get myself a home. I can cook, and make beds, and things. I could get a job on a farm somewhere. A sort of maid. . . ."

" Yes," said Uncle Tam heavily and sorrowfuly. " I guess you could do that, Carey girl. And it might come to that. It will be mighty hard for someone as gently reared as you. . . . And all your good clothes. . . . You'd have to buy some plain cotton things, and hard-wearing shoes. And learn to do your hair straight without having the hairdresser and the manicure person, and all those silk underclothes and things you've been used to. But I guess if it comes to that you could measure up like all the Frasers. Oliver here might be able to find you a job. . . ."

Now Carey knew that Uncle Tam was playing tricks. She knew for certain why he had taken her to Myers's to have her hair cut and dressed, and her hands done, and all the pretty clothes bought for her.

She couldn't give him away, of course, but apart from that she knew he meant that about not giving her a home any more. He wouldn't have gone to all this trouble if he hadn't meant to try and unload her on Oliver Reddin, her executor.

Before they had come to Two Creeks he had explained that years ago when her own father had lived on his farm down here in Western Victoria he had taught the young boy Oliver Reddin all he knew about dairy cattle and thoroughbred horses. Oliver Reddin, the boy, had followed

11

Reg Fraser about like a shadow and from him had learned to tell a champion from a near champion.

Reg Fraser must have figured it out that Oliver Reddin owed him something, and that Uncle Tam was too old to act as trustee for a young girl. That's why he had made Oliver Reddin executor, and not Uncle Tam.

"I could manage somehow . . ." she said slowly, looking down at her hands again because she was ashamed for Uncle Tam and did not want this tall angry handsome man to see it: or to feel she wanted anything from him at all.

"Don't talk rot," Oliver Reddin said shortly.

There was another long silence in the room. Then Oliver Reddin stood up and came round the desk again.

"Look, Miss Fraser," he said. Then amended it to "Carey." "Look, Carey," he said in a quiet exasperated voice. "You go down and join Tony in afternoon tea while I talk to your uncle." He went to the door and held it open for her. "Go down that long passage across the hall and follow the smell of new-made ginger scones. If I know those two women in the kitchen they'll have the biggest oven going to give Tony just what the little wretch likes best. I'll talk to your uncle. . . ."

"Thank you," Carey said as she went through the door. She stole a fleeting glance at Oliver Reddin, meaning to make it one full of pride and independence, but somehow the cold look in his eyes intimidated her. She was through the door and it was closed behind her before she could muster up her courage to attempt to return it.

As the door closed, her pride did come to her assistance. Somehow its closing did something to her. It was like putting her out in the cold, along with Tony.

"I'll never forgive you for that, Mr. Oliver Reddin," she said to the closed door. "But meantime I'll have some ginger scones just because I happen to like them, too. Then I'll go away and never darken your doorstep again."

This sombre phrase about darkening doorsteps gave her the right kind of courage and she went down the passage in pursuit of the scent of baking ginger with a firm step.

Inside the study Oliver Reddin was back in his chair behind the desk. He lit a cigarette. Uncle Tom comfortably packed himself a pipeful of tobacco.

"I kinda worked it out," Uncle Tam said. "What with

this big homestead here, or maybe that Melbourne house with your mother and sister there to look after Carey, you could give her a home for a while. So as she could get some culture, and all that sort of thing."

"Mr. Fraser," Oliver Reddin said, choosing his words slowly as if to make each one ring with worth for the purpose of reaching this old outback farmer's understanding, "if I presented my mother and sister with an eighteen-year-old girl they would think I had either gone mad or that I was thinking of marrying her."

"Well, a darned good idea that would be," Tam Fraser said affably. "What with her farm next to yours, and you having to do all the business of seeing it gets put in order, it would be the very answer to the problem."

"Mr. Fraser!" Oliver Reddin's voice was hard. "I am not looking for a wife. I am concerned only with carrying out my duties as executor and seeing the girl has some kind of start in life. If you don't provide her with a home I suppose I've got to find her one. Meantime . . ."

"Yes, *meantime*," said Tam Fraser. "Meantime can I leave her here with you for a day or two? I've got to go up the country right away and the hotel in Melbourne's no place to leave a young girl. . . ."

"Specially when you haven't funds to pay your account there. Why can't you take Carey up the country with you?"

"Because I'm letting my place this very week and going to live in the Wybong pub myself. As you said . . . no place for a girl. Anyhow I can't pay for both of us. Haven't enough money."

"Why can't you let Carey look after you on the farm?"

"Like this farm her father's left her, it's gone to wrack and ruin," said Tam Fraser cheerfully. "I've had my day. Now I'm going to live in the hotel where someone'll get my meals and look after me, and no bothering about a young girl that's bred up too gentle and ladylike to rough it in a country hotel."

"All right," Oliver Reddin said at length. "I'll think it over." He looked sharply at the bent old man sitting at the side of his desk. "But don't make any mistake about it. I'm not sending her to the Melbourne house to my mother. That sort of thing might have been done by bachelor trustees or guardians in the Victorian age but

13

it's not done now. The position would be regarded as ridiculous. She'll have to stay here."

Tam Fraser looked pained.

"You mean stay here? With only a couple of maids to chaperon? Carey's eighteen, I'll remind you. She's a young lady, not a young girl."

"I'll be driven to getting a housekeeper, I suppose," Oliver Reddin said bitterly. "I don't know what sort of a crazy place this is going to be. What with Tony . . . and now Carey."

"Oh yes, and by the way," said Tam Fraser with his voice full of meaning, "Just who is this boy? This Tony?"

"He happens to be the son of my horse-breaker. His father was killed two months ago breaking in one horse too many. His mother died some years ago."

"Hmm," said Uncle Tam thoughtfully. "What you intend to make of him? A horse-breaker like his father?"

"That's what the boy thinks. But I've no one here to look after him properly. See he gets his schooling. . . ."

"Ah," said Tam Fraser, pointing the stem of his pipe again at Oliver Reddin. "That's where Carey comes in. See it? Someone to look after Tony."

"In a bachelor establishment?" said Oliver Reddin with his eyebrows raised and his eyes cold. "You think of everything, don't you, Mr. Fraser?"

"Not me," said the old man, shaking his head and smiling guilelessly. "It was my brother Reg who thought of everything. He made you executor."

Oliver Reddin stood up.

"I'll see that you get some tea, Mr. Fraser, and then order the car in ten minutes. It will take you and Carey to the train. I'll make arrangements to have her brought out here late to-morrow afternoon. The sooner you're both out of that hotel the better." He looked closely at Tam Fraser. "I'll pay that hotel bill out of Carey's estate . . . up until five o'clock to-morrow afternoon. Understand me?"

"I understand all right. Oh, and by the way. Carey's run up something of an account at Myers's . . . you'd better look into that."

"An account? What sort of an account?"

"Clothes and things. You know what girls are. And she was brought up well-dressed and gentle like. Her father gave her everything. She wouldn't know how to go without those things, Oliver."

14

"She'll learn," Oliver said grimly as he went to the door.

In the breakfast-room just off the kitchen Carey and Tony were sitting at the table eating ginger scones and sipping tea from large half-pint cups.

"Yeah," Tony was saying with his mouth full. "He keeps sending me away but I keep coming home."

"Don't you want to go to school?"

"No. Specially not an orphans' school. I want to be home."

"Don't you mind if Mr. Reddin gets angry with you?"

"No," Tony said, swallowing hard and taking another scone. "I'm okay when I'm home . . . but he keeps sending me away."

"But you can't get on in life unless you go to school."

"My father never went to school. He never read a book. But he was the best horse-breaker in the country."

Carey nearly said, "But you want to be something more than that," but she bit back the words in time, remembering that Tony would think that an insult against his dead father.

"If you stayed here it would be okay," Tony said unexpectedly, looking at her over the edge of the big cup which he had now lifted with both hands. "I like you."

Carey smiled, showing her deep dimple in one cheek and her white teeth between her red lips. She had pulled off her hat and it now lay on a chair by the wall. The sun was filtering in through the window and it brought out red and gold lights in her hair. Her blue eyes looked with understanding at the scrappy self-contained little boy.

"I like you too," she said.

They had been there half an hour when a shadow fell across the doorway and they both looked up. Oliver Reddin was standing there.

He looked first at the boy, then at Carey. He looked back again at Tony.

"Well?" he said severely. "What am I going to do with you?"

"I can sleep down at the quarters with the other stablemen," said Tony complacently. "And I ain't going back to any school. Or to Mrs. Potts's or Mrs. Sewell's. I'm going to run away and come home wherever you send me."

"You can't possibly send him away," Carey said impetuously. "You haven't been an orphan, Mr. Reddin. You

15

couldn't know . . ." She stopped short. His eyes had met hers and were looking deep into them as if reading and diagnosing and dispensing.

"I'm sorry," she faltered. "I suppose it is not my business."

He did not answer her but turned again to Tony.

"You can sleep to-night in the spare room by the big storeroom. I'll see what I'll do about you to-morrow. Miss Fraser . . . Carey . . . you'd better ask Hannah to fix a room for you in the long hall."

Carey started up.

"A room for me?" she said. "But I'm going back with Uncle Tam."

"That's what I thought," Oliver Reddin said dryly. "I told him the car would be ready in ten minutes. However, your Uncle Tam thought otherwise. He'd just gone down the drive and across the home paddock . . . taking a short cut to the main road. He didn't show any sign of waiting for you."

"You mean . . . *he went without me?* You mean he's *gone*? And left me behind?"

"I mean exactly that. He's walked out on you, I'm afraid."

Carey sat down again. Her blue eyes went dark with the shock of Oliver Reddin's words.

"But he wouldn't do that to me?"

"I'm afraid he has done that to you."

Carey's eyes clung without understanding to Oliver's eyes. His showed no signs of relenting. One orphan left on his hands had been trouble enough. Now he had two.

Something was tugging at Carey's arm. After what seemed a long time she turned her head and looked down at it. It was Tony's hand.

"That's all right," Tony said. "That's always happening to me. Mr. Oliver taking me to some person's house, or a school or something. Then just walking out on me. You'll be all right here though. There's horses, and lots of cattle and some sheep. And there's fish in the creek when the waters come down from the mountains . . ."

His voice went on and on. Unconsciously Carey had put her hand on top of Tony's hand and held it there pressed against the flesh of her own young arm.

In a dazed kind of way she looked back at Mr. Oliver Reddin standing silent in the doorway.

16

"As Tony said . . . You'll be all right," Oliver said. "Only keep out of my way till I can think what to do with the pair of you."

He turned and went away. Carey could hear his footsteps going quickly and purposefully down the long passage.

Uncle Tam, she said under her breath, *you're a wicked old man, and you're up to something. But you should have told me.*

"You got some decent shoes?" Tony asked, looking down at Carey's delicate blue tapered shoes with the high slim heel. "I can show you where the foals run in the paddock behind the stable. They're due to be broke from the mares nowabouts."

Carey looked dazedly at her shoes.

"My goodness," she said. "I haven't anything. I mean anything except what I've got on."

She fingered the fine silk of her dress. She glanced at the fashionable little white hat lying on the chair.

"Hannah will lend you something," Tony said. "Hey, Hannah! You got something to lend Carey to wear? She's staying."

The maid came into the room from the adjoining kitchen.

"She's what?" she asked.

"I'm staying," said Carey. "And I haven't anything to sleep in."

"My, oh my!" said Hannah. "Wait till Miss Reddin hears of these goings on. What's come over Mr. Oliver? Your uncle staying too, miss?"

Carey shook her head.

"Who is Miss Reddin?" she asked.

"Mr. Oliver's sister," said Hannah. "She won't want any pretty young lady staying at Two Creeks just now." She shook her head from side to side, then began gathering up the tea things. "I'll see Mr. Oliver about what you're to wear to-night," she said.

Tony nudged Carey.

"Miss Millicent, that's Mr. Oliver's sister, is going to marry her girl friend to Mr. Oliver. She brings her out here a lot. That's what Hannah means. But you're nice. I shouldn't mind if I were you."

"Why should I mind?" said Carey, looking down at Tony. "I don't even like Mr. Oliver. And I'm not going to stay here any longer than I have to. You might like it, Tony. I don't."

17

Tony slid off his chair.

" Wait till you see the foals," he said. " Come on. Oh . . . I forgot. Those shoes."

" I can take them off," said Carey. " Back at home I often went across the paddock barefooted."

Oliver Reddin, standing at his study window, looked in amazement at the pair crossing the gravel track and ducking under the rails of the home paddock. Tony looked as he always did, but the girl running beside him, with her hair, full of red lights, flying behind her, wore a blue French silk dress . . . and had bare feet.

The anger and astonishment passed from his eyes and in their place was a look of sardonic amusement.

" It will be interesting to hear what Millicent has to say to *that*," he said to himself.

CHAPTER TWO

For the next two days Carey, except when with Tony, had been very silent and what Uncle Tam had called " docile." Underneath she wasn't docile at all. She didn't understand Oliver Reddin or the way his big luxurious homestead was run. She was amidst alien corn and was still trying to understand what had happened to her. Uncle Tam loved her, she knew. But why had he gone off without a word of farewell? The bad old man was up to something reprehensible again. The thing that worried Carey most was that she wasn't there to get him out of trouble.

She had worn her one beautiful silk dress all day yesterday with one of Hannah's cardigans. At night she had slept in one of Hannah's long-sleeved nightgowns. Carey hadn't known there were nightgowns like that outside of books.

When her trunk arrived Oliver Reddin, face still remote and cold, stalked into her room . . . something that would never have been permitted outback . . . and told her to sit down " over there " while Hannah unpacked it. He stood, hands in his pockets, and watched Hannah bring out Carey's dresses one by one.

There was the brown cotton one she had made herself ; brown so as not to show the dust when the willi-willies blew. There was a grey woollen one she had made three years ago, and which did not quite fit her now, but it had been very comfortable on the frosty nights of mid-winter, sitting before the fire in Uncle Tam's house. There were her heavy low-heeled shoes, rather worn in the sole. There were her underclothes, carefully and neatly mended, which were very plain and with which she had found nothing wrong until Uncle Tam had told the woman in Myers's to buy " those pinky, lacy frothy things."

When the last garment was out . . . a nightdress that had been made from a pair of blue rayon curtains given her by Mrs. Wilson, the storekeeper's wife . . . Oliver Reddin looked down at Carey.

There was nothing any girl could say to a man who had just witnessed the unveiling of her total possessions. Her eyes met his for a minute and then dropped down again to her hands in her lap.

" That will do, Hannah," Oliver Reddin said. " You may go now."

Carey was an outback country girl but she was not so remote from civilisation that she didn't know that Oliver had done the cruellest thing that any man could do. He had exposed the poverty of her possessions.

At that moment when the last garment, the nightgown made of curtains, came out and was folded and put on the bed, Carey Fraser grew up ten years.

While Hannah went out of the room, and closed the door behind her, Oliver stood in silence, looking at the girl.

" Carey," he said at length, very quietly. " Whose idea was this? Yours, or Tam Fraser's?"

Carey had to protect Uncle Tam, of course. He was such a silly old man, but such a darling.

" Mine," she said, looking up. " I wanted to come to Melbourne. And I wanted a good dress and—and all the other things that go with it." She was quite used to telling white lies to save Uncle Tam from disgrace. She looked at Oliver Reddin steadily out of her clear eyes.

Oliver moved over to the mantelshelf on the opposite side of the room from Carey. He leaned back against it, his hands still in his pockets.

" When did you know your father had left me executor of your estate?" he asked.

" Oh, a long time ago."

19

Quite clearly she saw now what Uncle Tam had done. Oliver's questions helped to throw a light. By coming under Oliver Reddin's roof and patronage she was taking a big step up in the world . . . so Uncle Tam had thought. She would be a rich man's protégée.

Now, to save Uncle Tam's skin again, she had to pretend it had all been her own idea.

The sooner Mr. Oliver Reddin understood this the better, because the sooner would he send her packing.

" How long ago?" came the cold, finger-pointing voice. " How long ago did you know your father appointed me executor?"

How long had it been since her father had been well enough to worry about his affairs? If she said " Five years " she ought to be safe. She was sure her father hadn't bothered about any business affairs for quite as long as that. She would have been thirteen at the time. Old enough to understand.

" Five years," she said. " Five years, I think."

She missed the glimmer of a sardonic smile that altered, momentarily, the expression on Oliver Reddin's face. He knew what Carey evidently did not know, that Reg Fraser, her father, had made his will only eighteen months before his death. There had been a former will that made old Tam Fraser executor. The girl could not have known five years ago that Oliver Reddin, wealthy grazier of Two Creeks, was to be her trustee.

" Where did you say you got those clothes you are wearing?" he asked. " Myers's, wasn't it?"

" Yes," Carey said in a quiet voice.

" Do you remember the name of the saleswoman who helped you?"

" It was—it was a Mrs. Wellman."

Oliver crossed over to the bed and sat on it while he lifted the telephone from its receiver on the bedside table and dialled a number. He sat with his back to Carey but she could see his reflection in the wall mirror on the other side of the room. He was looking down at the toe of his shoes. He didn't look so cold or angry with his eyes covered by his lids like that. He looked like a very handsome man, except for his mouth which was too straight and his brow which was too stern.

" Oliver Reddin of Two Creeks," he said. " I want a complete skeleton wardrobe for Miss Carey Fraser. Mr.

20

Tam Fraser of Wybong opened an account for her several days ago. I want the usual sets of clothes that are sent out to stations and farms by mail order. Two or three of everything, including a pair of low-heeled shoes that aren't too plain. Mrs. Wellman will have the measurements and will remember the young lady."

He put the receiver down with a small bang. Carey stood up.

"Mr. Reddin . . ." she began. She made a small gesture of protest.

He stood up and turned to look at her.

"You're in my hands now, young lady," he said. "You'll do as you're told."

He walked to the door and opened it. He turned.

"By the way, my mother and sister will be here late this afternoon. You'd better keep up that quiet innocent approach of yours. It is as successful as it is effective."

He went through the door, and closed it behind him.

Carey looked lovingly at her old working shoes. To-morrow, she would do what Tony had done . . . walk across the paddocks until she had walked home. It might take her weeks to get there, but get there she would.

What she would say to Uncle Tam when she did get home would take all those weeks of walking to compose!

Carey did not hear Mrs. Reddin arrive because she was so busy hearing *Miss* Reddin's autocratic voice in the hall below.

"Hannah! Have the cases taken in, will you? Tell William he may drive the car round to the garage. See that my mother is taken to her room to rest at once, will you? Where is my brother? We'll take tea in the drawing-room as soon as we have taken some of the travel stains off. Don't bother to come up with me. I presume my room is in order."

Poor Hannah! Carey thought. All those things to do at once. She had an urge to go and help Hannah and another to peep over the banisters to see this grand lady who was issuing orders in a highly cultivated voice that was just a little too loud and a little too authoritative.

Carey did not go into the big dining-room for dinner that night, not because her nerve had deserted her but because Tony had invited her to dinner with Mrs. Wackett, the wife of the head stableman at Two Creeks. Carey told Hannah but did not tell Oliver Reddin. After to-morrow morning she would never see him again so she did not mind how angry he would be.

Mrs. Wackett and Tim Wackett, the stableman, had wanted to know all about Wybong and Carey had told them everything . . . even about the horses which were no more than brumbies caught when young, broken in and trained by anyone who wanted another mount.

"Cripes," Tim Wackett had said. "What a country! Can get a horse for nothing. Anyone comes here to buy one of Mr. Reddin's foals better have the best of five hundred pounds in his pocket. Stud stock we got here. Say, Miss Fraser, your dad used to run good horses over there at Wintall. That fellow who was runnin' it for him sure took him down a heap. Pity your dad was a sick man."

"Do you mean that over on my farm we could have good grazing like Mr. Reddin's got here? Green grass? And we could irrigate from the creek?"

"Sure. Oliver Reddin's always clapping his eyes on that place and wishing it was his. I've heard him say many a time he wished he could open up our racing paddock and carry it out over the long paddock at Wintall. But it 'ud cost a fortune right now. There's bracken all across it. An' plenty of blackberry, too."

"But if it was Mr. Reddin's it would pay him to have it cleared, wouldn't it?"

"Too right. First-class investment. You thinking of selling it to him, miss?"

Carey did not answer for she was really thinking not of " selling " it to him but of " giving " it to him. That would pay him for that hotel bill and the Myers's account, not forgetting her own board and lodging for three days.

Tony had yet another idea.

"Me and you could farm that place, Carey," he said. "You could bring some of those brumby foals down from Wybong and I could break 'em. Like my dad . . ."

Even Carey laughed for she too knew that stud stock meant generations of breeding, and brumby stock had no breeding at all. But the idea brought a light to Tony's eyes.

"Which would you like most, Tony? To be my horse-breaker, or my manager?"

"Both," Tony said promptly.

"All right. You get some schooling so you can keep

the account books as well as the stud books . . . and I'll make you my manager."

"Yes . . ." said Tony dolefully and kicking the table leg with his boot. "That means going away again. I'm not ever going away from home again. Not ever . . ."

He looked balefully round at the three pairs of eyes watching him.

"Two Creeks is his home," Mrs. Wackett said sadly. "It would break his heart to go away."

"Mr. Reddin would let you come home for holidays, wouldn't he, Tony?" Carey asked.

"How would you like to be away from your home?" Tony asked stonily.

Something squeezed at Carey's heart.

"Yes, Tony," she said sadly. "I think home is best after all."

How could she preach to him to-night, and to-morrow know that he would throw her advice to the winds when he found out that she too was quite a hand at *running away*?

Up at the homestead, dinner over, Millicent Reddin was sitting in one of the button-backed chairs pouring the coffee for her mother and her brother. She was tall, perhaps twenty-nine or thirty years old. Her yellow hair was dressed high on her head in what she called a "Paris roll" and at the back it showed the nape of a long haughty neck and in front a clear square brow, not unlike her brother Oliver's brow except that she was as fair as he was dark.

"I never heard of anything so absurd in all my life," she said in her clear hard voice. "A girl of eighteen left in a will to a man. *Any* man, let alone a bachelor. What on earth kind of a girl can she be, dining now down at the stables."

"Not at the stables, dear Millicent," Oliver said. "At Tim's cottage. Quite a different thing. Though, by the way, my stables are kept fit for a king to dine in. She was not left to me in a will. Her affairs were."

"The same thing surely if the girl is sent here like a parcel done up in string from the never-never."

"Perhaps she might be useful on the estate, if she's from the outback," Mrs. Reddin said hopefully.

Her daughter cast her an oblique look.

"If you can't get rid of her, that is a possibility," she conceded.

"Why should I want to get rid of her?" Oliver asked lightly. Until that moment he hadn't had a clear idea what he would do with Carey. He was surprised in a slightly ironic way at finding himself her champion. It was a curious fact that Millicent always inspired him to take the opposite point of view.

"It's a pity that nobody milks cows these days," Mrs. Reddin said. "It's all mechanical, of course. Otherwise she might . . ."

"An executor does not put his protégée to work as a domestic servant on his own property, Mother," Oliver said. "He merely looks after her affairs. There's no occasion for Carey to stay here or go from here. It has nothing to do with the facts of the matter . . . where she stays. She just happens to be here at the moment. I'm glad you were both able to come out to Two Creeks because obviously she couldn't stay here for long under any other conditions."

"Were you thinking of keeping her for *long*?" queried Millicent, astonished.

"I had thought of asking you and Mother if you would take her into the town house for a period. Until Carey herself decides what she wants to do."

Millicent ran a finger along the inside edge of her necklace.

"Well now . . ." she said. "Of course you are asking something. Not that one would mind ordinarily. That is, if it was a *man,* or a *child*. But a girl of eighteen! I ask you, Oliver! How would we account for her except by saying she is your responsibility? Then you know what people would say. They would simply shriek with laughter at the idea. You have your friends to consider, Oliver. And my friends, too. What do you suppose I'd say to Jane, for instance?"

"Ah, yes . . . Jane," said Oliver. Neither his mother nor his sister heeded the irony in his voice. "Jane's opinion is, of course, important."

"She is my best friend. And yours, too, Oliver. You never had a more loyal friend, and admirer, than Jane Newbold. What's more she's recognised as the beauty of Melbourne society."

"Yes, Oliver dear," his mother said. "We often wish you would marry Jane. She is a dear girl, and Millicent would be so happy."

"That, too, is important," said Oliver, with an ominous quiet in his voice that was completely missed by the other two.

"What does this girl look like, Oliver?" asked Mrs. Reddin plaintively.

There was the sound of a distant door opening and shutting.

"I think she is coming now," Oliver said, getting up. "I'll bring her in. You can see for yourselves."

He went out into the hall. Carey was just turning into it from the cross passage. She started when she saw Oliver.

"Come into the drawing-room, Carey. I want you to meet my mother and sister."

Carey was surprised at the seeming kindness in his voice. She looked quickly up into his face to see if he meant it. He looked away as he took her coat and put it across a chair in the hall.

When he straightened up and turned he made a gesture for her to precede him to the drawing-room. His whole manner seemed to have changed. He was courteous, almost as if she had been an honoured guest instead of an orphan left on the doorstep by Uncle Tam. She entered the drawing-room with a greater calmness than she herself realised.

"My mother . . ." said Oliver Reddin, making the introductions. "My sister Millicent."

Both ladies inclined their heads. Carey smiled delicately. Then she looked at Oliver for direction.

"Sit down, Carey," Oliver said, placing a chair for her. He stood behind it and held it for her as she sat down. "Millicent will give you some coffee."

He crossed the intervening space to the coffee table and waited while Millicent filled a cup with the rich brown fluid. He carried it, with the cream jug and sugar, to Carey. He looked at her hands, not her eyes, as she helped herself.

"Thank you," she said, glancing up, offering a fleeting nervous smile.

His eyes were no longer cold, though they were still impersonal. Strangely, she felt that he alone, in that room, was a friend. Was it only because she already knew him, and the very silence of the other two cast up a barrier between them and her?

"Of course she is very young, Oliver," Millicent said at length, addressing her brother and not Carey.

25

"Eighteen," Oliver said. "You are eighteen, aren't you, Carey?"

Carey nodded. She could not say anything because she had just taken a sip of coffee that was too hot.

"Very pretty for an outback girl," said Mrs. Reddin. "You do come from the outback, don't you?" she asked.

Carey nodded.

"Wybong." She wished her voice hadn't squeaked. And she wished she didn't have that dreadful compulsion to look at Oliver for support.

"Her hair is nearly the same colour as Jane's . . ." said Millicent. "Of course Jane's hair is so luxuriant and really red. And always in place."

"But it is a lovely colour, as you implied," said Oliver.

What were they doing to her, thought Carey? Walking all round her with their thoughts, like the stockmen looking over a horse or a bullock before they bought, or even made a bid.

"She is very quiet, you will notice," Oliver said, looking at his mother. "Her uncle, old Tam Fraser guarantees she is docile."

A flush began to steal up Carey's cheeks. How dare they do this to her?

"That makes it so easy," said Mrs. Reddin. "I do believe, dear . . . yes, I do believe . . . we could have her for a little while in the town house. What do you think, Millicent? Not if you don't wish it, of course, dear."

Oliver rubbed his hand across his chin. His glance, edged with a sardonic gleam, passed from his mother to his sister. It did not miss the fact that his sister had affected a bored expression but that really she was relieved to find Carey so mouse-like, so quiet.

"I'm glad of that, Mother," Oliver said. "And I'm glad you like the look of Carey. You see, with Carey's permission, you are looking at my future wife."

Carey did *not* drop her coffee cup. Her eyes moved away from Mrs. Reddin and Millicent to Oliver. Uncle Tam, she thought, was not the only man who was full of tricks. Carey did not know that the difference between Uncle Tam and Oliver Reddin was that Uncle Tam planned his deeds, cunningly, long before he committed them to action. Oliver Reddin made up his mind in a flash and seldom had occasion to regret the accuracy of his judgment.

26

If Carey was for him the answer to Millicent's dictatorship she was also the answer to the problem of Tony . . . and the occasional embarrassments of a bachelor household. She was glowing with youth. She could be amazingly beautiful if she was taught how to do that wonderful hair . . . and to dress.

Oliver Reddin did not believe that any man's actions were motivated by love. Love was an illusion and had very little to do with the realities of life. But a young and beautiful wife had its attractions.

Oliver showed nothing of these thoughts as across the room he observed the look of dazed astonishment in his sister Millicent's eyes.

The problem would be one of training Carey for the role, of course! However, as Tam Fraser had said, she was *docile*.

CHAPTER THREE

In the morning Carey did not run away for the simple reason that at eight o'clock, before she had finished breakfast with Tony in the little room next to the kitchen, Oliver had sent for her.

Oliver's command was not to be denied. There was nothing for it but to follow Hannah down the long passage, across the hall to his study.

He stood up as she came into the room, walked round the big square table and indicated the chairs under the window. They were those she and Tony had sat on the day Uncle Tam brought her to Two Creeks.

Oliver pulled his chair forward and turned it at an angle so he could see Carey.

"Did you sleep well?" he asked.

When she had sat in this room before she had thought him a cold man, but terrifically impressive. Now she thought him just as impressive but no longer so very cold. He was not as friendly and affable, laughing and joking, as Harry Martin at Wybong, perhaps; but he was quiet and strong-minded, something she liked in a man.

"Yes, thank you," she said, and she looked down again at her hands in her lap.

"Don't do that, Carey," Oliver said abruptly. "It is

a very pretty gesture, especially as you carry your head well. However, the lowering of eyes on the part of young ladies went out with the Victorian era."

Carey raised her eyes to meet his.

"Didn't you know?" he said, his eyebrows raised quizzically.

"If I had thought about it," she said slowly, "I guess I would have known that." She thought for a minute. "I wasn't doing it as a gesture, Mr. Reddin. I was doing it to pass the time. You see, I didn't have anything to say."

"Oh, indeed? Why didn't you have anything to say, Carey?"

"Because you wouldn't understand me, Mr. Reddin, any more than I understand you."

There was a look of surprise in his clear grey eyes as he looked at the girl now.

"You thought it would be wasting time talking to me? Your executor? The man who is to look after your affairs?"

"Yes," Carey said simply and truthfully.

"I see!" Oliver said carefully. "Then what did you think of my statement to my mother and sister last night? That I intend to marry you?"

"I didn't think about it at all," said Carey and remembered just in time not to let her eyes drop to her hands in her lap.

"Why not?"

Carey smiled.

"It was a silly thing to say. Besides . . . I hadn't thought about getting married just yet."

"You hadn't thought about it? Then you'd better think hard now, Carey. Because that is the best possible thing for you. And incidentally it will be useful to me."

"Why is it the best thing for me?" Carey asked, surprised in her turn.

"Because you haven't got a home. Or any visible means of support. At least not until we put that farm next door in order. And that will take some time."

"Oh, I can support myself," Carey said, with a smile. "You see, I can work. I've always worked at Wybong. My uncle used to paddock the horses for the stock plants coming into town for a rest-up after the pay-off . . . and I used to look after them. I used to look after the men too when they'd spent all their money. They would come and camp on our veranda and I would cook. . . ."

28

She stopped short as if alarmed at herself doing so much talking.

There was an ironic gleam in Oliver's eyes.

"That is what your uncle calls being gently bred, I suppose? Being brought up as a lady? Caring for euchred stockmen after they'd bust their cheques wide open at the local store?"

Carey's head went a shade higher. Her small round chin was very firm and her blue eyes looked directly into Oliver's grey eyes.

"We never sat in a room called a drawing-room, Mr. Reddin. It was just the 'sitting-room' where I come from. But everyone talked to the stranger . . . and never talked about her while she sat there and listened. I would have thought that a very unladylike thing to do, and no one in Wybong would have done it."

There was a slight smile at the corners of Oliver's mouth.

"You've touched home there, young lady. Incidentally I apologise for my mother and sister. You see . . . they were very worried. On your behalf."

"On my behalf?"

"Exactly. Where we come from young ladies do not live alone in a bachelor's household."

"But I'm not alone. There's cook, and Hannah and Tony."

"Ah, yes. There's Tony."

Oliver sat silent a minute then he got up and went across to his desk and took a cigarette from a silver box. He lit it and walked to the window. He stood looking out thoughtfully.

Carey watched him, and marvelled that a man could look ready for work out on the property yet be so well-groomed.

Yes indeed, he was terrific to look at, Carey thought. Underneath, however, he was proud and hard and selfish. And a little intimidating. When she did get back to Wybong she knew she would love to tell people . . . especially the girls . . . about him. But just now she would concentrate on his faults, not his virtues.

If Carey had been thinking over Oliver's points, he had certainly been looking over hers.

She had beautiful, little, endearing features with that round chin of hers, the short straight nose and the clear brow. Her eyes were frank and honest, too . . . if just a little dreamy.

29

She mightn't be as quiet and malleable as he had first thought. She had some spirit. Well, that would be all to the good if Millicent tried to run her the way she persistently interfered and tried to run Two Creeks, its staff and even Oliver himself. A little spirit could be an asset.

Through the window Oliver watched Tony running across the bottom of the garden.

"That boy needs schooling," he said unexpectedly.

"You mean Tony?" Carey asked. "But he's very homesick away from Two Creeks."

Oliver turned towards her. He did not sit down. He seemed to look down at her under lowered eyelids.

"If you married me would you be prepared to see that Tony goes to school regularly and learns to dress himself decently, and behave like a little gentleman?"

"Oh, yes," Carey said eagerly, not thinking about marrying Oliver but about looking after Tony. "He's a clever little boy, isn't he?"

Oliver nodded his head.

"Clever as they come," he said. "I'm not going to see him waste his life as an illiterate roustabout on Two Creeks. His father was a fine man and first class with horses. But Tony is something more. . . ."

Talking about Tony, the difference and antagonism between them had fallen away. Carey was just a gentle soft-hearted girl talking to a hard-hearted man about an orphan boy who had as many brains as he had qualities of spirit.

Oliver sat down again and leaned forward towards Carey.

"Could you run this homestead and keep Millicent at bay?"

Carey put her head on the side and thought. When she came to think of it she had managed her father, who was very sick and very difficult. And she had managed Uncle Tam, who was a naughty tricky old man. She had even managed some of those stockmen when they had come over to Uncle Tam's veranda to sleep off the last of their leave. She had looked after their horses, had mended their clothes and even cut their hair.

"Yes," she said thoughtfully. "Yes . . . I could manage Millicent."

She looked up. Oliver was watching her face, his eyes intent.

Oh, how handsome he was now! Yes . . . he was terrific.

30

When she got back to Wybong she would fill all the ears with tales about him. . . .

"Good," Oliver said. "Then we'll get married as soon as possible. You should go to Melbourne first and get some grooming. It will have to be a big St. Kilda Road wedding, I'm afraid. That's something I can't get out of. . . ."

"Oh, but I wasn't thinking of marrying you. I was thinking of going back to Wybong."

"Then you think again. You're going to marry me, young lady. And soon."

Carey's mouth opened as if to say something, but the words died unuttered. Oliver was standing up, and he held out his hand to her. It was a commanding gesture more than a friendly one.

Mechanically she put her hand in his and he drew her up.

"You add it up, Carey," Oliver said. "Six for you and half a dozen for me. And Tony can have the run of Two Creeks."

"But . . ."

"There are no buts. Now this is what you are to do." He dropped her hand and went to his desk. "I'll make arrangements for you to go to Melbourne to-morrow. I'm going to send you to a Mrs. Cleaver for a fortnight. In that time she'll teach you how a big home like the Melbourne house is run: about the servants and how to handle them. She'll equip you with clothes and arrange the wedding from your side." He looked up, "She'll attempt to do something about your accent but on that score you have my permission to skip the homework. I like the slow soft drawl as learned in Wybong."

"Mr. Reddin . . ." began Carey.

"Oliver, please. You are addressing your future husband. Unless you want to continue all your days as purely Victorian."

Carey let her lashes droop on her cheek as she looked side-ways and down at her hands.

"And if you do that again I'll slap you," added Oliver.

He didn't know that this time Carey had done it on purpose. Just to punish him for calling her Victorian. Little did *he* know how much a young girl could learn about life in Wybong!

All that day Carey lived in a daze. She did not see Mrs.

Reddin or Millicent that morning because they were break-
fasting in their respective beds and Tony was waiting for
her outside the breakfast-room adjoining the kitchen.

"Come on quick," he said. "We're going to Ballarat.
Tim Wackett is taking us in the station wagon. He's going to
see about some horseflesh he's bought from a pastoral agency
there."

"Don't I need a coat of something?"

"No. There's always a rug in the wagon. Anyhow the
back part is closed and heated. Say, Carey, what's the matter
with you? You aren't listening."

"Yes I am. I'm . . ."

"You aren't worrying about anything Mr. Oliver says,
are you? You don't want to take no notice of him, Carey.
If he gets up steam all you got to do is walk away and
hide out down the creek or some place round the stables
for a day or two. Then he cools down."

"That's what you've been doing all your life, Tony, and
that's why you say ' don't take no notice of him.' If you
stayed up at the homestead or went to school you would
learn to speak properly."

"Or soft and drawling like you? Come on. Let's run
down here. You got those comfy shoes on?"

He looked at Carey's feet and nodded approval at the
stout warm shoes that had come with her own clothes
from Wybong.

"Let's run," he said again. And run they did.

Carey sat in the back of the station wagon while Tony
sat in front with Tim Wackett and discoursed on the condition of the properties they passed. When they passed horses
grazing near the paddock fences both he and Tim Wackett
ceased paying attention to the road and nearly fell through
the window taking in and discussing the points of this horse
and that gelding.

All along the creek beds the willows were shooting.
The blue gums stood around in silent clumps and the grass
was so green Carey could have squeezed the green out of
it in drops ; if she could have gathered the grass in her hands.

No wonder poor Tony wouldn't stay where he was put
. . . if all this freedom and all this glorious countryside was
denied him.

As for herself! What did marrying Mr. Reddin mean
exactly? It was very strange how she found it almost an
accomplished fact when she hadn't really thought about it

at all. It was as if her mind was already made up for her.

The real implications of being married to Oliver Reddin simply did not occur to her. She thought, when she was able to think, about living all her life in that beautiful old homestead and in the middle of all these vast green fields! Of always being able to run along the creek bed with Tony; rambling over her own farm.

Except, of course, for going to Mrs. Cleaver for a fortnight. That, Carey visualised as being a continuous lesson lasting fourteen days on how to walk down a long room on a chalk line, like the stockmen did on the veranda back home when they were trying themselves out after a bust-up and waiting for the station owners coming into town to recruit mustering teams.

She thought of Oliver as " Mr. Reddin " and she still thought about telling the girls back in Wybong about him. Adding, of course . . . " And what do you think? I *married* him!"

Ballarat was a beautiful city. Great lines of trees made a garden of every main street even in the very centre of the business area.

Tim Wackett set Tony and Carey down by Lake Wendouree and left them in the gardens to their own resources while he went about his business.

Carey sat on a seat and gazed at the bronze images of the country's prime minsters. Tony, bursting with the restlessness of a very young boy, lost patience with her.

" You just sit and stare," he said. " Say, what's the matter with you to-day, Carey?"

" I was thinking of Harry Martin. He was a man I knew back in Wybong. I was wondering what he would think about my marrying Mr. Reddin."

" Cripes! You're not going to marry Mr. Oliver, are you? I thought you were just another orphan like me?"

There was disillusionment in Tony's voice. He had been cheated. Carey was a wolf in sheep's clothing. She belonged to the class of people who sent him away and made him go to school.

" I won't ever let you down, Tony," she said, knowing instantly what he felt by the note of sorrow in Tony's voice. " It will be just the same between you and me. It will mean I can stay at Two Creeks without Mrs. Reddin or Millicent thinking it isn't proper."

" What do you mean ' isn't proper '?"

Carey shrugged.

" People are like that in this part of the country. If I stayed in the house alone with Mr. Reddin they might think we were sweethearts."

" And won't they think that if you're married?"

" People don't think about married people at all," said Carey. " When you're married you're finished. I mean finished with people. They don't bother about you any more. They just let you alone."

" Marry Mr. Oliver," said Tony sagaciously. " Then we can go down the creek any day we like. Besides, Tim Wackett will have to give you a good mount. Millicent always gets the best on the place."

" Tony . . . would you get me a drink of water . . . or something?"

" Are you feeling bad, Carey? Look, I've nothing to carry the water from the tap to you. Have you got sixpence and I'll go to that shop and buy a cool drink."

" No, Tony," said Carey sadly. " You see that's the trouble. I haven't even a penny, let alone a sixpence. That's why I'd better marry Mr. Reddin. I was going to walk home to-day. But seven hundred miles is just a bit far, whichever dress I wear."

" Well, if you can walk over to the fountain I'll help you, Carey."

Carey stood up. Slowly she straightened herself. It was funny how much comfort there was in a little boy's shoulders. He put his small arm around her and guided her as if she was an old blind woman.

" Tony darling . . . you are a dear," she said. " I'm so grateful for you. It's wonderful to have someone— someone to help me." She had been going to say " Some-one to love " but remembered in time that that sort of thing was likely to embarrass a small boy who, being manly, was above sentiment.

She bent over the fountain and splashed the cold water on her face. Then she cupped her hands and took a drink.

Yes. She had better marry Mr. Reddin. It was the answer to such a lot of questions. And there would always be Tony at Two Creeks.

Late that afternoon Carey's new clothes, ordered by Oliver from Myers's, came by express delivery.

There weren't a great many clothes but there was a dress for every occasion: a morning dress of polished cotton, and a woollen jacket that matched it. There was another silk afternoon dress. And there was a pearl-coloured lace dress with blue flower buttons and a taffeta underskirt that was too lovely for Carey to do anything with but finger and gaze upon. That was for the evening. There was a pair of black suéde shoes with pointed toes and a bow and the heels, though delicate and moulded, were only of medium height.

There were two pairs of shortie pyjamas and two slips . . . and three of everything else that went next to her skin. There were three pairs of stockings and three pairs of gloves . . . all different colours. There were some lace handkerchiefs and some plain handkerchiefs. There was a complete make-up kit.

"How did they know what to send, and how many things?" Carey asked Hannah.

"That's their Station Service," Hannah said airily. "Sometimes people right from the very centre of Australia or even the far north want what is called the 'skeleton wardrobe' with which to come to Melbourne or Sydney. If the store has the right measurements this is what they send. Then when people arrive in town they've got something to wear at once . . . so they don't look too outback . . . if you know what I mean."

"Now, of course, I'm fit to go to Mrs. Cleaver's," said Carey.

"Well, that'll be nice," said Hannah.

I hope it is, thought Carey and she allowed herself a little impish laugh that she had been able to toss her head at the idea of staying with Mrs. Cleaver. In actual fact she was very nervous about it. Mrs. Cleaver, she imagined, would be much more terrifying than Millicent.

CHAPTER FOUR

Carey made no more discoveries about the terrifying part of Millicent that night for Oliver drove her, Carey, with Tony up along the Hume Highway, then north through the mountains to the Log Cabin at Mount Macedon for dinner.

Carey wore the new silk dress that had come that afternoon, and the new black suède shoes that, though they looked as dainty as the other pair, were more comfortable because the heel, though slim, was not quite so high. All the same, she reflected, she would not want to walk seven hundred miles in them.

Some inner instinct told her that marrying Oliver was the sensible thing to do to put everything in order. It settled the matter of her father's farm which under the will Oliver had to administer; of Uncle Tam who wanted to live at the hotel where he had no more domestic troubles, and of Oliver who wanted someone to care for Tony and to settle the problem of when he would marry and who he would marry. Sooner or later he would have to have a wife . . . for convenience sake.

She was very young, yet she had the confidence of a young girl who had had to manage a sick man, a foolish uncle and all the itinerant stockmen who had used Uncle Tam's house and paddock as a stamping ground for themselves and their mounts when they came into town after the pay-off.

The only thing she did not visualise, and did not attempt to visualise, was what happened next . . . after the wedding ring was slipped on her finger and she changed her name for Oliver's name.

She told herself it meant looking after Tony, and keeping Millicent from running Two Creeks against Oliver's will.

Up the gullies and round hairpin bends the great car swept, and eventually pulled in to a stop outside the Log Cabin.

Inside a great log fire was burning. The dark wooden tables were set with coloured striped cloths and the cottage chairs standing around put the last rural touch to the cabin.

Oliver selected a table by the window overlooking the valley. Already night was closing in so that all they were likely to see through the window were the stars beyond the mountain peaks.

He consulted the menu and ordered the dinner, then he turned at last to Carey and Tony. He looked from one to the other.

" I believe he thinks we are both children," thought Carey.

Underneath his brusque manner he must be a kind man, though. A cruel man would have turned both herself and Tony away, and would have sold the farm as it stood. She felt a little warming of gratitude towards him because of

36

his sense of honour in dealing with responsibilities that had been wished on him by other people.

However, he quickly dispelled this illusion.

"The first thing you will have to do, Carey," he said across the table, "is teach Tony some table manners. With those he is wearing to-night we are not likely to enjoy our meal."

"I've seen worse table manners than Tony's," said Carey truthfully and loyally. "Nobody round Wying gives the wandering stockmen cups and saucers because they always drink straight from the billy. . . ."

She broke off because Oliver was looking at her with an odd expression in his eyes. Suddenly she remembered Uncle Tam telling him she had been reared gently . . . as a lady. Uncle Tam had deceived him, and Oliver Reddin knew it. He thought she too had been party to this deceit but was so inept about it she kept giving herself away.

Oliver Reddin broke straight into another subject without any comment on what Carey had just said.

"I will take you into Melbourne to-morrow," he said in a businesslike way, as if the whole matter of preparing Carey for marriage . . . and marrying her . . . was the same thing as a business undertaking. "We will go straight to Mrs. Cleaver's house. I have already been in touch with her by telephone and she understands the whole situation." He paused. "I want you to put yourself entirely in Mrs. Cleaver's hands, Carey. As a matter of fact I feel you are wise enough and . . . shall we say inexperienced enough . . ." this with a touch of irony, "to know that it is the best thing. She will tell you exactly what is expected of you. She will arrange your clothes and your outings. When she thinks the time is suitable she will take you to Cranston in the St. Kilda Road. That is our Melbourne house. My mother and sister are returning there the day after to-morrow. The wedding will be arranged from the church of which the family have always been parishioners; and the reception will be at Cranston. We will remain at Cranston for several days, and then I'm afraid we will have to return to Two Creeks. The racing season is just beginning and I have been pasturing several racers. I have to be on the property."

Carey ate her fish with care, nudging Tony when he picked up the wrong knife or fork, and by using her eyes directed him to the right ones. If Oliver noticed this unspoken conversation going on between the young boy and the girl he proposed to make his wife, he said nothing.

Carey, with her quiet inward smile, thought Oliver was probably surprised she knew herself which knife and fork to use and when.

Uncle Tam was right in spite of what Mr. Reddin thought. She *had* been taught proper social usage at Wybong. Her father had been a gentleman, and a pastoralist, in his days of good health himself. Mr. Reddin seemed to have forgotten that.

Now she had to be sent to Mrs. Cleaver to learn to be a lady! Carey hoped very much that she would get on with Mrs. Cleaver.

Oliver had taken out his pocket-book.

"To-day is October the third," he said. "On Thursday October the sixteenth I will call for you at Mrs. Cleaver's house. I will take you home to Cranston. We will be married on Saturday, October the eighteenth."

With an unexpected thud of her heart Carey saw that that wedding wasn't something in the distant future at all. She had a sudden panicky feeling. She did not look up at Oliver but rather down at Tony sitting beside her. The small boy looking up saw the bleak expression in her eyes. He jogged her left foot with his right foot to let her know he was there; that he understood and that between them they would thrash out all difficulties.

Oliver sensed the contact between the two and he put down his pocket-book and looked at them.

"Carey," he said quietly. "You do know what getting married means?"

Her eyes flew up to meet his.

"Yes, of course, Mr. Reddin. I've seen lots of people married at Wybong."

"Would you please call me Oliver. Don't let me tell you that again. And I think the sooner you forget what you saw and learned at Wybong the better. You are in a different tract of country now."

"Yes, I do know, Mr. . . . Oliver. The paddocks are so green and they're so big. . . ."

"And the people are different."

"Oh yes, the people are different," agreed Carey. But she was careful not to say that in an argumentative way. Oliver Reddin was not a man with whom one argued. Besides, she had seen where arguing had led her Uncle

Tam. Now, if Uncle Tam had only learned to keep quiet at the right moments! Like Tony, for instance.

The roast duckling and apple-sauce was before them now. Tony had been served with a drum-stick and he was about to pick it up in his fingers when Carey nudged him with her elbow. With a sigh Tony took up his knife and fork instead.

Carey looked up to see if Oliver had noticed. His eyes were studying her with a strange look of concentration.

"Do you think you could grow up in two weeks, Carey?" he asked, with a slight touch of exasperation.

"I grew up a long time ago," she said. "I just don't look like it on my outside. But inside . . ."

"Yes. I wish I knew just exactly what does go on inside that head of yours."

"You'd be surprised," Carey said quietly.

"The young can sometimes be very wise," Oliver said unexpectedly.

"Am I wise?" Carey asked, pleased.

"Very," he said with a sudden sternness. "You are wise enough to marry me without making a fuss about it. You will be looked after for the rest of your life."

"And my farm will be looked after, too," said Carey. "You will be able to open up the racing paddock and run your horses right through my place, too, won't you, Oliver?"

His eyes studied hers for quite a long time. He shook his head slightly as if rejecting an unwanted thought.

"That would be to the advantage of us both, Carey. You know that, don't you?"

"Yes, I figured it out," said Carey.

"We all figured it out," said Tony. "Me and Tim Wackett, too. You could train 'em for the Melbourne tracks on a long run like that, Mr. Oliver."

"I'll have something to say to you and Tim Wackett when I see you down at the stables in the morning, young man. For the time being get on with your meal, and speak when you are spoken to. Moreover, if you touch Carey's foot again I'll put you outside."

Anger had settled in his eyes and Carey wished she hadn't raised the subject of the farm. If that was what Oliver wanted the farm for it surely didn't matter if he said so?

"You can have the farm, Oliver," she said impetuously. "You see, we'll be married. And what's mine is yours."

Oliver's eyes went very dark.

"The first thing Mrs. Cleaver can do is take you to a lawyer," he said. "You will be informed that an executor is in a special category that does not permit him to make any gain personally from an estate he administers under a trusteeship. Do you understand that, Carey?"

"I didn't, but I do now," she said.

"Good. Then when you have finished your dessert, and when Tony has resisted the temptation to lick his plate as well as his spoon we will leave. We will drive into Melbourne as early as possible in the morning."

Mrs. Cleaver's house was a dignified villa set decorously in a lavish garden, well screened from the road by a hedge of hibiscus. Oliver's car swung up the short drive-way and came to a stop below the veranda. A gardener materialised from the recesses of a shrubbery and began at once to take Carey's case from the boot of the car.

As Oliver, taking Carey's arm, went up the steps and crossed the wide porch-like veranda the front door opened, showing an impeccably capped and aproned maid.

"Is Mrs. Cleaver at home?" Oliver said. "I think she is expecting Miss Fraser. Will you please tell her she is here . . . with Mr. Reddin of Two Creeks?"

"Will you come inside, sir. Mrs. Cleaver is expecting you in the small drawing-room."

They were ushered into a pretty room towards the back of the wide hall. A very attractive-looking woman, in her late forties, rose from a chair by a square occasional table and came forward to meet them.

She was of medium height, with hair, black just going grey, set in curls resting on the crown of her head and of which there was not one hair out of place. She wore a simple dark charcoal grey dress of heavy silk which was so simple there was nothing but a piece of material to it. Yet it was the most elegant thing for that hour of the day Carey had ever seen.

Mrs. Cleaver smiled in a friendly way that both charmed yet maintained a distance.

"How do you do?" she said. "Please do come in. I hope you have had a comfortable drive in from the country?"

With a gesture of first one hand then the other she indicated where Carey and Oliver were to sit.

Having smiled again at Carey, she sat down, crossed her feet at the ankles and not the knees, put her hands in her lap where they continued to look a decoration and not an embarrassment, and turned to Oliver.

"I'm delighted to meet you again, Mr. Reddin. It is some years since we met, isn't it? Shall we agree the years have been kind to us both?" She smiled again as if in some pleasant conspiracy with Oliver. "I am so glad you brought Carey to me. I shall look forward with great interest to arranging her wedding for her."

Carey knew she had received in those first few minutes her first lesson in deportment and demeanour. Every gesture and each word had its own private dignity so that Carey felt warmed and welcomed, yet not invited over the doorstep that divided the purely private from the purely public life of Mrs. Cleaver.

Sitting there, her own hands in her lap, unable to think what to say, Carey breathed a little prayer that when, in that far distant time, she was as old as Mrs. Cleaver, she would look like her and behave like her . . . in all times and places.

Mrs Cleaver's dark eyes took Carey in without appearing to do so. "Mr. Reddin, we must get down to business. I understand your wedding is to take place on 18th October. In the meantime Carey is to be introduced to some activities in Melbourne . . . the Elizabethan Theatre, the Symphony Concrt . . . Opera? Benjamin Britten's *Peter Grimes* is to open next week, by the way. Some plays? Am I right? Then, of course, there is a wardrobe to be arranged. I'm afraid that is likely to take up a lot of our time unless we get a designer to call here. Would you like that, Carey?"

Carey glanced swiftly at Oliver. Mrs. Cleaver was quick to notice this inquiry on Carey's part.

"The child hasn't any money of her own . . . or any will of her own, probably," she thought. "He's found a sweet inexperienced pretty girl somewhere and wants me to make her ready for marriage in a fortnight. These *men*."

She leaned forward and pressed a bell button in the wall over the square honey-coloured table. She did not wait for Carey's answer to her last question.

"This sort of occasion is always spoilt by business, Carey," she said lightly. "I'm going to ask Myrna to take you to the sun-room where two other young ladies . . . both from outback . . . have just finished having their hair set and

41

their manicures. They will look after you while I talk to Mr. Reddin."

All three rose. Again Carey looked across the room to Oliver for direction. What should she do now? Just go outside with the maid . . . if that was who Myrna was?

Oliver stood, tall and silent, and nodded his head slightly at Carey.

"I think that would be a better arrangement," he said formally.

"Say good-bye to Mr. Reddin now, will you Carey," said Mrs. Cleaver lightly. "I'm so very sorry I never allow private partings, even between engaged couples. You see, we all lead a kind of exaggeratedly formal life here. Rather convent-like in that respect, I'm afraid. But all my old girls tell me later that it makes their release out into the world so much more exciting. And the strictness and formality here proves such a wonderful defence. Almost an *armour,* they tell me."

The maid had arrived at the door and Mrs. Cleaver made a signal to her with her hand. The maid stepped aside as if waiting for Carey to precede her out of the door.

Oliver came across the room to the door. As Carey turned to go he held out his hand. She put her hand in his.

Mrs. Cleaver did not know, of course, that there had never been any partings between herself and Oliver, private or public. If there was a flush in Carey's cheeks now she would think it was because she minded saying good-bye to Oliver here in the little drawing-room.

And she did mind saying god-bye to him.

Perhaps it was because leaving him was like cutting a painter. He was the only person she knew, the only person with whom she had any personal tie or connection seven hundred miles south of Wybong.

"Good-bye, Oliver," she said in a low voice.

"Good-bye, Carey. I will call for you at four o'clock on Thursday, 16th October. If you need anything will you please let me know?" He was grave, formal, and distant.

With an infinitesimal sigh Carey turned and followed Myrna from the room.

Mrs. Cleaver turned back to her chair and as she sat down she said:

"Now, Mr. Reddin, will you let me know what the

position is, please? You understand it is essential for me to know as much as possible about you both in order to make Carey happy . . . as well as to prepare her for her marriage?"

"You want the blunt truth, Mrs. Cleaver, so you shall have it. I'm a busy man with a big property on my hands and a lot of Shire commitments. The problem of getting married has nagged at my mind for some time. When Carey was left on my hands it occurred to me she might be the answer to that problem. She is a very pretty girl and there isn't a man alive who wouldn't feel that was quite an important qualification . . . if not, of course, the first."

He stopped and looked directly at Mrs. Cleaver.

"I think something could be made of her," he went on. "She is good material. Comes of reasonably good family, has a lot of common sense . . . some spirit. I will confess I decided on the spur of the moment but I have not regretted my decision."

"Then I take it that this is not . . . at this stage . . . a love match?"

"I think there is a lot of boloney talked about love, Mrs. Cleaver," Oliver said, with a cold note in his voice. "Living a lifetime together amicably is much more important, and encompasses that emotional state in a well-suited match surely?"

Mrs. Cleaver had been presented with this situation very often in her career as a " finisher-off " of young ladies. The outback man has too often to make his marriage arrangements this way.

What surprised her was that Mr. Reddin, whose property was not so far distant from the capital, and whose family had considerable connections in Melbourne, had not been attracted to someone in his own immediate circle

Thinking of Carey during the few moments she had seen and spoken with the girl, she thought she could see what had happened. The girl had arrived in his life at a crucial moment when he was thinking he ought to get married. She was pretty, very sweet, and with a hint of character? Youth was, of course, her greatest asset. It made her malleable to a masterly mind like Mr. Reddin's.

She saw Mr. Reddin's point of view. A great deal could be made of Carey. A rich and fairly powerful man could afford to make, to his own order, the woman who would ideally suit his background.

"I see," she said noncommittally. "I am quite clear as to the situation and I think you will be quite happy with Carey when she leaves me." She stood up. "I expect you are a busy man, and I won't detain you."

Oliver rose, and they moved together toward the door.

"I hope," she said very gently, "that Carey also will be very happy." Then before Oliver could reply she added. "I'm to draw on your accounts with your pastoral agency, I understand?"

"As much as you think necessary," Oliver replied. "I want Carey to *look* the part. That is essential. My wife has a considerable position to maintain in the Shire. Frankly I'm not so interested in the city social whirl."

"She shall be everything you expect in that respect, I promise you."

Carey found the table conversation most difficult. It all had to be "small talk." The art of conversation was not the art of being interested on one topic, Mrs. Cleaver said, but being able to ask the right polite question that would get the right polite reply . . . and yet would allow for a change in the topic two sentences further on.

Carey thought she would never learn the art of conversation easily when it was so much easier to take refuge in silence.

"But I'm not really silent inside myself," she explained to Mrs. Cleaver. "I'm noticing things and thinking about things and even saying things . . . inside myself."

"Of course. We all do that. But outwardly we must make some attempt to put the other person at his or her ease. That is the great test. Is your companion at ease with you when you are silent . . . talking inside yourself?"

Each afternoon a different girl was hostess to their formal afternoon tea parties and each evening a different girl ordered and arranged the menu for dinner. Every morning was given up to face massages, hand-grooming, and the dressmaker.

She went shopping with Mrs. Cleaver at George's in Collins Street and to the smaller select shops in the arcades. She bought dresses and hats and shoes and ornaments; handbags and gloves and beautiful underclothes. She bought the most beautiful little pink hat in the world. Carey loved it so much she would have liked to take it to bed with her.

At the moment she wished to go on staying with Mrs.

Cleaver for ever; for ever getting ready, talking about the great day, preparing for all those impossible social impasses that might occur in the life of a young girl marrying a pastoralist with a big Melbourne house and a social position as well as a grazing property near the mountains.

"I do hope Oliver doesn't have to pay for all these things," Carey told Mrs. Cleaver one morning when they had done a lot of ordering in George's in Collins Street. "I do hope my own farm will pay for most of them. . .."

"Don't talk about what things cost, or who will pay for them," Mrs. Cleaver chided. "It's not polite, my dear child. But, of course, you must never buy indiscriminately unless your husband agrees."

Carey felt more startled than chided.

My husband.

Those actual words had not occurred to her before. They were away at the back of her mind and she had been avoiding them.

She said nothing and Mrs. Cleaver, thinking the girl might be hurt by the rebuff, tapped her hand gently.

"For the moment, Carey, we have no worries, dear. Mr. Reddin has arranged with his pastoral account to see that you are fully equipped. . . ."

"Oh yes, I know," Carey said hurriedly. "But I do have a farm, you know . . . Mr. Reddin is my trustee."

"Do not refer to him as Mr. Reddin, Carey. You must always refer to him as you speak to him as 'Oliver.' On rare and formal occasions you may say 'my fiancé' and later, of course, 'my husband'."

"I see," said Carey. "It's just that he is such a stranger. And so much older than I am. Do you know, Mrs. Cleaver, he must nearly be double my age."

They were returning to the house in a taxi. Mrs. Cleaver was silent for quite some time.

"Carey," she said at length. "You do understand what marriage means, don't you? Your engagement does seem to have been so very short, and engagements are generally a period during which two people get to know one another and get close to one another. It is like a preliminary to marriage. It smooths the way. I have been just a little worried about the distance between you and your fiancé. He does not appear to have written to you, nor you to him."

"No," said Carey. "I didn't know what to say to him. I suppose he doesn't know what to say to me."

45

Mrs. Cleaver suppressed a sigh.

"You haven't a mother, or aunt, have you? I feel that you might need someone to help you with advice. Carey . . . you would ask me if you were troubled about anything, wouldn't you? I mean . . . are you sure you know just what marriage means? You have to share your life in every way. Sometimes it is not easy with someone who is almost a stranger. . . ."

Carey was silent for a moment.

"I know there is a big gap between me and—and Oliver," she said with a sudden sad note in her voice. "Somehow we have to get over it, don't we? But nobody else can do it for us, can they? We'll be so alone. I mean, after we are married. . . ."

Mrs. Cleaver touched her hand.

"Yes, dear. That is what I mean. If ever I can help, you will ask me, won't you? Don't think that when you leave me on Thursday you have left me for ever. You will still belong in part to me. I will always be here."

Carey knew if she needed Mrs. Cleaver she would always go to her. It was wonderful to think she had someone else in Melbourne, besides the Reddin family, as friend.

The following afternoon she had to be taken to tea at Cranston with Mrs. Reddin and Millicent. In the morning she had gone with Mrs. Cleaver to the jeweller's to have her finger measured for her wedding ring.

Carey, standing in the jeweller's shop, closed her eyes and wished she could wake up one month hence. Then it would all be over . . . an accomplished fact. The difficulties, the embarrassments, the strangeness of being Oliver Reddin's wife would all be things of the past. She would be back at Two Creeks, running down the creek bed with Tony, walking over the grasslands of her own farm.

CHAPTER FIVE

Cranston was an awesome house. It was big and intimidating in its dignified seclusion behind a high hedge off the St. Kilda Road.

Apart from surprise at the size of the house, Carey had a nervous feeling when she realised that in three days' time she would be present here at her own wedding, and that somewhere or other in it she would sleep as Oliver's wife. There was also the problem of meeting again Mrs. Reddin and Millicent.

The thing for which she was totally unprepared was Jane Newbold's presence.

She was so striking with her dazzling figure, her clear-cut imperious features, her arched brows and perfect bow of mouth that Carey stared beyond Millicent's approaching figure with nothing but dismay in her heart.

But why didn't he marry her, she thought, bewildered. For she knew it was Jane long before Millicent uttered the not-very-magic-name.

" Oh, here you are at last," Millicent said in her quick staccato manner. " Come and meet Mother."

Carey thought it sounded as if they had not met before. This kind of drawing-room approach to social intercourse was all double Dutch to Carey. If Mrs. Cleaver hadn't been beside her and so making her conscious of all the " don't's and do's " of afternoon tea parties she would have failed to smile and look composed and *feel* composed.

All the time the greetings were going on Carey was conscious of that tall glamorous figure standing by the window and watching the new arrivals with a faint smile of amusement on her lips.

As Mrs. Cleaver shook hands with Mrs. Reddin, Millicent said:

" And now Jane." As if this was the special present out of the bon-bon box. " Jane . . . this . . . *this* is Carey."

" How do you do?" Carey said, shaking hands. " I'm afraid I'm not sure of your other name."

" Jane Newbold. But I imagine it is simpler if we use our Christian names, don't you think? We're bound to see so much of one another."

Carey noticed that Jane's expression of tolerant amusement had subtly changed. She was looking at Carey closely as if trying to find some fault . . . some flaw.

Mrs. Cleaver had seen to it that Carey's appearance was faultless. She made a charming picture. Mrs. Cleaver had seen her natural possibilities at once and had not tried in any way to put a veneer over Carey's personality.

Carey smiled now at Jane Newbold, and only Carey knew that for once her smile had been automatic and did not come from the heart. Jane Newbold was not her friend. Those probing eyes were looking for reasons as to why this girl was in the Reddin house at all, let alone as the future bride of the only son.

"Thank you," Carey said to Jane's suggestion about the use of Christian names. "I'm called Carey."

"I'm sure I'd never be able to say it like that . . ." Jane said, with a laugh. "Car-eey! Goodness . . . quite a pretty drawn they have outback."

Mrs. Cleaver was already sitting down near Mrs. Reddin and they were discussing the wedding arrangements.

Since no one had asked Carey to sit down she now crossed to a chair near Mrs. Reddin. She could not go on talking to Jane in this manner. She would like to be friendly but not even in Wybong would she let someone try to make her look silly in front of other people.

Mrs. Reddin looked from Mrs. Cleaver to Carey.

"Yes . . . you are a pretty girl, Carey," she said. "I thought so the first time I saw you . . . only you had such quaint clothes on. All wrong. A blue silk dress and the oddest shoes. . . ."

Carey smiled.

"That's all I had with me except two dresses that were even funnier than the silk one. But I'm the same person whatever dress I have on. . . ."

She really smiled now for she saw she had broken through Mrs. Reddin's reserve. The older lady's eyes brightened. She looked quickly at Millicent and then back to Carey.

"You have quite a sense of humour, dear."

She stopped short as Millicent came towards the tray.

"Do pour the tea now, Mother," Millicent said. "I'm sure Mrs. Cleaver is dying for a cup of tea. And this is the first meal Jane has in the day."

"Oh," said Carey. "You have not been ill, I hope?"

"No," said Jane, faintly bored. "I merely look after my figure. At your age, my dear, I'm surprised you don't have to worry about accumulating puppy fat. I suppose hard work has kept your figure under control?"

Carey knew just how she would have retaliated to that one if it hadn't been for Mrs. Cleaver's presence and Mrs. Cleaver's standards. She was thoughtful a moment. It really wasn't worth while making wise retorts to Jane. It was so much easier not to do so. And she didn't want to make an enemy of someone who was Millicent's friend.

"Yes, I have worked hard," Carey said simply.

Mrs. Reddin handed a cup of tea to Millicent who carried

it in one hand to Mrs. Cleaver; in the other she held a lovely little silver bracket holding the silver milk jug and sugar bowl.

"That's what I said to Oliver," Mrs. Reddin said brightly. "So useful to have someone on a station who can work hard. In my day the women weren't just decorations. We had to . . ."

"That was in the past, Mother," Millicent said so sharply Carey felt sorry for Mrs. Reddin. She could see Oliver's point about Millicent. She was too bossy and even Mrs. Reddin bowed to her daughter's strong personality.

"Yes, dear, I'm sorry. Of course times have changed. And Oliver is so much wealthier than your father."

"Mother, is this Jane's tea? You have poured it too strong. I'll ring for Bessie to bring another cup."

"Yes, dear, and you might ask Bessie to take Carey to see the suite of rooms we've set aside for her and Oliver . . ."

"There's time enough on Thursday for that." Millicent had pressed the wall bell with a vigour that must have informed Bessie in some nether regions that all was not well with the tea-tray in the drawing-room. Millicent came towards her mother again. "You might as well pour Carey's tea while we are waiting."

With great self-control Carey prevented herself from flushing or looking towards Mrs. Cleaver. In those simple disdainful words Millicent had disposed of Carey as the least important of the guests.

Millicent, Carey could see, would take quite as much tactful management as Uncle Tam.

When they rose to leave, Mrs. Reddin held Carey's hand warmly. She looked as if she might have kissed her except that when she glanced quickly at Millicent her daughter gave an almost imperceptible shake of her head.

"Well dear . . . we'll see you on Thursday. It will be so lovely to have Oliver. Usually we have to go to Two Creeks to see him. There's one nice thing about having a daughter-in-law . . . we can have a wedding, and perhaps see Oliver more often."

"Mother . . . Mrs. Cleaver is waiting to shake hands with you."

"I'll say good-bye now, too, Mrs. Reddin," said Jane. "I'm afraid I'll have to go, *darling*," she added to Millicent. "It's Lady Carson's do to-night. I'll see you there, won't I? Everybody's going, of course."

"May we give you a lift?" Mrs. Cleaver asked Jane pleasantly. "We have ordered a taxi."

"No thank you," Jane said. "I have my own car. Do you mind if I leave ahead of you? I haven't been watching the time. I was so very interested in seeing Car-eey." She laughed lightly and mockingly as if the way Carey said her name was a joke.

Carey smiled. For the sake of the Reddin family, and Mrs. Cleaver's standards, she would offer the other cheek. But she firmly hoped that in future years she wouldn't see too much of Millicent's friends.

Thursday was, in one sense, the day of days. After it, Carey thought, the wedding could almost be an anticlimax.

For fourteen days she had been wondering, day and night, what Oliver really looked like. Somehow his picture had faded in her mind. She knew, as she got up, bathed and dressed on Thursday morning, that she wanted to see Oliver very much. She wanted to see *whom* she was marrying.

She wondered what it was that had made her think on the first day she had met him that he was "terrific." Now she only knew theoretically that he was a lot older than herself, very striking and handsome but she couldn't remember why or how.

Thursday morning went quickly because, after packing, Carey had to have a session first with the hairdresser and manicurist and then a final fitting for her wedding dress.

After lunch Mrs. Cleaver insisted she lie down and have a rest for an hour.

"Promise me you will rest as much as possible to-morrow at Cranston. Early to bed both to-night and to-morrow. I'll tell Mr. Reddin myself. A bride should always look lovely and refreshed."

Carey's mind couldn't leap that far. Her heart beat so fast she was sure she would never rest.

Oddly enough she did sleep. The morning had been tiring . . . especially the standing when her wedding dress had been fitted. She lay on her bed and watched the tracery of leaves patterned by the sun on her window-pane. The next minute Myrna was touching her.

"Wake up, Miss Carey. I've brought you a cup of tea. It is just after three o'clock, and Mr. Reddin will be here at four."

When she had finished dressing she stood in front of the long mirror and looked at herself.

The porter came in and took her cases away. The maid came in and took away the tea-tray but paused to look at Carey and smile.

"You do look lovely, miss . . ." she said. "I do hope you'll be happy. And come back and see us sometime."

"Thank you, Myrna. Yes . . . yes, of course. I will come back." .

Then quite suddenly she didn't want to see Oliver at all. She wanted to stay here, safe and cared for, away from his cold executor-like manner. He wasn't the man she was going to marry at all. He was the executor who was giving her a home.

She looked in the mirror and saw that the colour had flown from her cheeks.

What if she slipped out the side door and went back to Wybong?

If she did slip out the side door where would she go in this biscuit-coloured suit with the pretty hat and shoes that had cost the earth? Where would this sort of clothes take her in the world of Melbourne's wide busy business thoroughfares?

There was a light tap at the door and Mrs. Cleaver came in. She noticed Carey's pallor but she did not mention it. Instead she sat on the bed and touched the girl's hand.

"It is rather a nervous ordeal . . . after fourteen days without seeing one another, isn't it? But you'll find it worth it. There is so much fresh and new to see in one another. Although I do not allow ' partings ' in private, I certainly allow reunions in private. In fact they are essential, aren't they?" She looked at her wrist-watch. "Five minutes to go," she said. "If I know Mr. Reddin's reputation he will be punctual. I'll go down and meet him in the big drawing-room, Carey. I'll send Myrna up for you in a few minutes."

As Carey turned towards her she leaned forward and kissed the girl lightly on the forehead.

"All happiness to you, my dear," she said. "I know you are going to be happy."

She smiled and in a minute had gone out of the room.

Carey walked to the mirror and looked at herself again.

"It's only Mr. Reddin," she told her image reflected there. "You don't have to be scared of *him*. Not after

51

what you've been through up at Wybong. Men? Why, you could write a book about the kind of men that come in off the stations after pay-off way back there!"

All the same she couldn't see herself putting Oliver to bed after he'd had a spree. She couldn't see Oliver having a spree at all.

Besides, bossiness was Millicent's privilege.

Thinking of Millicent gave her courage, and at that moment Myrna tapped at the door.

"Mr. Reddin is in the drawing-room, Miss Carey. Mrs. Cleaver will see you presently in the back drawing-room."

"Thank you, Myrna," Carey said.

She wondered if it was really herself that was walking carefully and gracefully down the broad carpeted staircase, through the wide hall to the drawing-room door. She seemed to be looking at herself from the outside and saying . . .

"My, you're a pretty girl in that new hat and those blue shoes! Not a scary-cat either. Must be Millicent who's brought the Fraser battling blood into circulation again."

In the open doorway she paused.

Oliver Reddin was standing by the window looking out on to the lawns and garden beds. He turned. An expression too fleeting to capture sprang into his eyes. Then it was gone. Carey wanted to put out her hand and capture it for she wasn't sure it didn't have the iridescence of a soap bubble. But it was gone and she knew she would never know what it was, or what it had portrayed.

"Well, Carey," he said. "You look well. Have you been happy with Mrs. Clever?"

She came across the room to him.

"I don't just look *well*," she said, smiling. "I look *beautiful*. I mean for *me*. Do you like my dress . . . Oliver?" She found it quite hard to get out that *Oliver*.

There was a faint ironic smile in his eyes now.

"Very much," he said. "Stand here in the light and let me look at you."

"Do you like my shoes, Oliver?" Carey asked, looking down at her feet. Her lashes rested on her cheek and though she did not know it that fleeting expression not unmixed with pain and pleasure passed over his face again.

"Yes, I do like your shoes, Carey. But you haven't got over that habit of looking down, have you? Tell me,

52

why do you do it? So that I can admire your long lashes?"

Carey's eyes swept up to his face.

"I didn't expect . . . or want . . . you to admire anything about me, Mr. Reddin . . . I mean *Oliver*."

"Oh? And why not?"

Carey extricated her hands from Oliver's light grip. She turned and looked out the window.

"I don't really know," she said. "You see, I've never met anyone like you before." She glanced at him again. "We don't really know one another, do we? I mean you don't know *me*?"

"Not the real you. But we've time to learn. Come, shall we go and say good-bye to Mrs. Cleaver? I believe the porter has put your cases in my car. A trunk has already arrived at Cranston."

"Are we going to Cranston now?"

"Not immediately. I'm going to take you to tea first. The sooner we get to know one another the better, don't you think? And you must have an engagement ring, you know."

Carey wondered why he always had that wall of distance and cold reserve between himself and other people.

All the same she felt happier. He really was "terrific" to look at. Fancy Carey Fraser from Wybong marrying anyone like Oliver Reddin of Two Creeks! She wondered just what it would be like.

CHAPTER SIX

The wedding was a Hollywood dream as far as Carey was concerned. The church, at the end of the road, was full of people, and Cranston was so bedecked with flowers it was like Flower Day in jacaranda time.

There were hundreds of people . . . or so it seemed to Carey. The women were most beautifully dressed and wore small hats with roses round them and long flowing dresses. As they passed they left a faint perfume on the air, and they were all smiles and surprise and whispers at Oliver Reddin's enchanting little bride.

Uncle Tam had come down from Wybong to give her away. He almost strutted in his new dress clothes; and he twinkled with glee every time he thought how clever he had been, getting this fine husband, this great home, these high-flown society people for little Carey.

"Couldn't be better pleased if I'd won the Melbourne Cup," he told everyone as he shook hands at the reception. "Very kind of the Reddins to lend us their house for the wedding. My station at Wybong is too far away . . . and of course Carey's farm is not yet in order."

Carey sighed but smiled. She was grateful to Oliver that he had brought Uncle Tam to Melbourne . . . and that he accepted silently the nefarious scheming of this gay but irresponsible little old man from the outback.

Then she saw Jane Newbold. She was so elegant, so exclusively dressed in a beautiful brocade gown and a peacock blue hat that had small gilded lilies round it! Everyone turned and looked and nodded a head and said, "Ah, *Jane*. She really is the most beautiful creature alive."

Of course Uncle Tam fell the first victim to Jane's beauty. She led him away into a corner, ordered champagne to be brought to them and sat down to examine Uncle Tam on the subject of life at Wybong.

"Of course you're proud of your niece, Mr. Fraser." She smiled. "I'm surprised the young men of Wybong hadn't snapped her up long ago."

"There was always Henry Martin the contractor," said Mr. Fraser stoutly. "Everywhere Carey went Harry Martin took good care of her. He was *very* fond of her. Very, very fond."

"And now she's left him with a broken heart." Jane laughed gaily. "What a thing it is to be young!"

"Smashed to smithereens," said Uncle Tam. Then, remembering to defend Carey against the charge of cruelty, he quickly added, "Of course Carey loved him, too. Why, they couldn't be separated. But what's a fellow in a country town for the niece of a station owner, Miss Newbold? I couldn't possibly allow it, now could I?"

"Of course not. And Oliver Reddin would be such a very desirable match. I expect you worked that out very carefully." She tapped his hand gaily. "Very clever of you, Mr. Fraser. What a fairy godfather of an uncle you turned out to be!"

"Why not? Carey's only got one uncle. Up to me to do something for the girl, you know."

"And being young, she and this . . . this Harry Martin . . . will get over it?"

"Of course, of course. Why, he's planning to come down to Victoria to look at that farm for her. That's one of the jobs I've got to fix while I'm down here myself. See that Oliver takes on Harry Martin to organise the place. A better worker never lifted a muscled arm. Besides, there's nothing he'd stop at to help Carey."

Carey, standing under the arch in the great reception room, wondered if Oliver beside her noticed that gay *tête-à-tête* in the corner. She closed her eyes in a little prayer that Uncle Tam would see that Jane Newbold was not a person to whom one unburdened one's heart. And why didn't he see she was too beautiful, too much in demand really, to be wanting to spend the whole evening talking to an elderly man from outback!

She glanced up at Oliver. How different he was now! He was being friendly and charming to everyone. It was as if something in him had thawed out. Or was he putting up a front to convince all these people this wedding was born in heaven and destined for a paradise on earth?

She wondered if he liked her in her wedding dress. She wondered what he thought about her at all.

She wondered what it would be like when he kissed her. For he had not kissed her yet.

Hours later the wedding was over, yet now it all seemed to have passed in a flash.

Carey had taken off her wedding dress and come back in a pale primrose lace evening dress. The lights from the chandelier overhead brought out the red lights in her gold hair. She stood beside Oliver and said good night to everybody.

When the last guest had gone Millicent said:

"You two had better go up to your rooms. After all, it is your wedding. I'll see to the servants. Well, Mother dear, I think we managed everything satisfactorily. Now we've got time to talk about everyone. Oliver, did you see how marvellous Jane looked? She really did outshine everyone."

"That is Jane's destiny, surely," Oliver said. "I would be disappointed if Jane didn't do exactly that." He turned to Carey. "I'll come to the top of the stairs with you, Carey, then I'll come back and have a glass of wine with my mother." That small tell-tale ironic gleam was in his eye. "After all she has just lost her only son to another woman," he added.

In her room Carey undressed, and after bathing put on her pink satin dressing-gown. Was this what one did while one's husband was having a last glass of wine with his mother?

Did she go to bed, or did she wait up? If only her long-lost mother could speak from the grave and tell her what to do next! And why hadn't she asked Mrs. Cleaver?

She was tired; and anxiety had drained the colour from her cheeks. The more uncertain she became, the more the shadows of weariness darkened under her eyes.

There was a tap on the door and before she could answer it, it opened and Oliver came in. He closed the door behind him and as he came in he saw Carey standing in the middle of the room, her face so white, her eyes with dark rings around them, she might have been on the point of fainting.

Quietly he came across the deep pile carpet. He put his hand, the one carrying the gloves, on Carey's shoulder and with the other tilted up her chin.

"Carey," he said sharply, "are you *afraid* of me? What sort of person do you think you've married that you should stand there looking so white-faced; as if you are expecting an ogre?"

He shook her shoulders slightly.

"Answer me," he said. "Are you afraid of me, Carey?"

Yes . . . she was afraid. Not of him, but of being awkward, stupid, embarrassed. She wanted to do everything simply and easily, and she didn't know how to go about it. Nor did she know that if he had put his arms round her then the worries would all have resolved themselves in that warm comfort.

"Yes," she said in a low voice. "Yes, yes." She brushed her hands across her eyes as if they hurt her. Why didn't she know what to do?

Oliver dropped his hands to his side.

"If that's the sort of person you think I am . . ." he said evenly, then stopped. He walked around the room, then came back to where she stood watching him, her face paler than ever. Tears for her own ineptitude were shining at the back of her eyes. He put out his hand and tilted her chin up and looked at her again. His own eyes were dark.

"You had better grow up some more, Carey," he said with a touch of bitter weariness in his voice. He turned and went to a second door. "I have a room next door," he added. "If you want anything . . . I will be here. But I assure you, you have nothing to *fear*. I'm an ordinary human being, not a brute, Carey. I would not *harm* you."

Carey stood unable to move or utter a word.

Perhaps he didn't want her, after all. He only wanted to find a home for her and find someone to learn to run Two Creeks. That accounted for his cold manner. He didn't really want her, Carey, as his wife at all. Was that it?

Whatever he did or didn't want, right now he was a tired angry man, and he was quite indifferent to how she felt.

Yes, she would go to bed . . . the only unkissed bride in history. For the truth of it was Carey had never been kissed by boy or man . . . not even by Harry Martin.

Carey had indeed been very tired, yet she did not sleep well, Oliver's attitude on the previous night left her with the bottom knocked out of her world. She was hurt that he had not bidden her a generous or kindly good night.

Why, oh why, hadn't she run away to Wybong just as Tony had run away to Two Creeks? Had she . . . unknown to herself . . . *wanted* to stay?

When she had first sat in that study with Uncle Tam and looked at Oliver Reddin she had looked down at her hands in order to think in privacy so the open candour of her eyes would not tell the tale of her thoughts.

Her heart had welled in excited wonder at being in Oliver's presence, and at finding the executor her father had named was this striking well-dressed man with an air of authority.

"Yes," Carey thought, burying her face in her pillow on her wedding night, "I thought he was ' terrific.' That was it! That was the real truth of it! I stayed because of *him*. Not because of this big house . . . or the big wedding . . . or because Two Creeks is green and rich and so beautiful. Not even because of Tony."

Well, she would show him that she didn't seek any emotional overtures from him whatever. She would not be a clinging wife. He would receive in return from her just as much as he gave. At the moment he gave her a home, and Tony. Her home and Tony was all that she would care for herself.

Two Creeks, and yes, her own farm.

Uncle Tam had said something about Harry Martin coming down to help with the farm.

She and Harry and Tony! Yes, together they could get on with the farm. With Harry's help that too could be made to blossom the way Two Creeks blossomed.

Thus her thoughts went on and on between dozes, all through that night. Early in the morning she fell into a heavy exhausted sleep.

It was eleven o'clock when she awoke. Oliver, fully dressed, came into her room.

He stood at the foot of her bed.

"So you are awake, Carey," he said. "I thought it was time to call you. I've decided to return to Two Creeks this afternoon. Will that disappoint you?"

Carey was barely awake for it had been the sound of Oliver coming into her room that had disturbed her.

"Two Creeks?" she said dazedly. "Yes . . . I want to go to Two Creeks. And to my farm. Now we can begin to put my farm in order, can't we? I mean now that I'll be living at Two Creeks we can begin to work on my farm. Harry Martin is coming to help me. . . ."

Vaguely, for a moment, her thinking and disturbed dreaming of the night was all one with the reality of the morning.

"And Tony," she said with a little more eagerness. "One day Tony could manage the farm for me . . . when he is grown up."

Oliver stood at the foot of her bed and looked at her.

"Is this your form of building castles in the air, Carey?" he asked. "Your farm . . . Tony . . . this Harry Martin? Is that what you have been thinking?"

Carey was wide awake now. She pulled the sheet up high under her chin.

"Yes," she said firmly. "I know just what to do now. I've a great many plans. . . ."

"And that's why you married me?" he asked with an edge of sarcasm in his voice.

"Well, there were two reasons," Carey said thoughtfully. "You asked me first . . . no, you didn't. You *told* me to marry you. I thought it would please you. The other reason was the farm, of course."

Oliver Reddin appeared to look at her curiously.

"And which are you going to put first? Two Creeks or your farm?"

"Two Creeks," said Carey without hesitation. "You see, that will be my duty. . . ."

"And the farm your love?"

She nodded. All sleep was gone from her now. She was wide awake. That is what it would have to be. It could have been so different if he had kissed her last night . . . if he had begun to warm to life a spark of love between them. Whatever else he thought, he must never, never be allowed to think that she had felt something deep and stirring in her heart about him.

Carey offered a half-smile over the edge of her sheet at Oliver.

"If you wouldn't mind going outside now," she said quietly, "I will get up and get dressed. I suppose you've had breakfast long since."

"I have," said Oliver dryly. He had looked amused and then annoyed when Carey had suggested his going outside. "I told the maids to leave you to sleep. I'll ask Ada to bring you in some tea now and then you might come downstairs for lunch at one o'clock. My mother and sister are remaining in their rooms as they are exhausted after yesterday's celebrations. Ada can help you pack."

"Thank you," said Carey.

Her blue eyes, quickly veiling the sadness that was in them, watched him turn and walk over to the door.

Perhaps if she smiled when he turned round . . . It was so very hard to play at being something that wasn't truly herself. She was older than her years or her looks . . . if only he realised it.

But he did not turn round. He put out his hand behind him and shut the door.

Carey lay in her bed looking at the closed door. She bit her lips to prevent them trembling.

Lunch, Carey decided, was a silly affair. She decided this so as not to let herself grow sadder or to spoil the lovely day outside.

Oliver sat at the end of the dining-room table and she sat round the corner on his right hand. Every time the maid came into the room Oliver talked to Carey about various people who had been at the wedding. When the maid went out of the room he fell silent. Trying to match her demeanour with his, Carey fell silent, too.

"It is necessary to be polite and courteous to all these

people if and when we meet them again," Oliver said of the wedding guests. "You won't be seeing much of them after we return to Two Creeks. I spend most of my time on the station. The Reddin family is an old Melbourne family and for the sake of tradition . . . as well as for Mother's and Millicent's sakes . . . I uphold some of the customs and keep the social ties. Hence the size of this wedding."

He paused, lifted his head and looked down the length of the dining-room towards the window as if the patterning of sunlight and shadow in the trees outside had drawn his attention.

"Christenings, weddings and funerals," he added, with a touch of the sardonic. "They are the events that keep us all together."

Immediately after lunch Oliver made arrangements for their departure. Cases were put in the boot of the big car outside the main entrance. A station wagon was to follow with Carey's new trunks and other cases.

Carey went upstairs to say good-bye to Mrs. Reddin and Millicent, and to thank them for all their trouble over the wedding.

"Don't thank me, my dear," Mrs. Reddin said from the pillowed recesses of her bed. On a table beside her was a great silver tray with covered silver dishes. She had had her lunch brought to her in her room. Millicent, now sitting in her satin dressing-gown in an arm-chair, had shared it with her there.

"If we didn't have a wedding . . . or something like that . . . it wouldn't be worth keeping up this big house. Sometimes I think . . ."

"You shouldn't think so much, Mother," Millicent said. "This house is our home. It is a symbol of our position in Melbourne."

"Yes, dear, but all the other big homes in the St. Kilda Road are being bought up for schools or hotels. . . ."

"*Mother!*" said Millicent sharply as if to chasten a blasphemy. She turned quickly to Carey. "You are to see that Oliver does nothing about selling this house," she ordered. "It is the Reddin home. It must never be a school or a hotel. . . ."

"Is this house Oliver's house?" Carey asked innocently.

There was a momentary silence.

"Didn't you know?" asked Millicent with a sudden wary note in her voice.

Carey shook her head.

"I don't know what is or isn't Oliver's," she said. "But I'd never ask him to sell anything he values. Or that you and Mrs. Reddin value."

"We value everything in it," said Millicent. "If you were to alter things you would cause my mother great unhappiness."

Carey felt as if she had stepped unexpectedly on an ants' nest.

"I don't think that is a bit likely," she said. "You see, Oliver likes Two Creeks best. So do I. He also likes to retain his Melbourne connections. He told me. So I feel sure Cranston will stay just as it is. . . ."

She could see the stiff defensiveness gradually seeping out of Millicent's erect figure.

"As long as Oliver thinks that way it will be all right," Millicent said. She looked at Carey steadily out of a pair of eyes made hard by anxiety and suspicion. "You do rather look the kind of person who will be guided by Oliver," she said at last. "I'm sure we'll all get on very well together as long as you don't . . . well . . . don't upset us here at Cranston."

"Yes, dear," Mrs. Reddin said. "I don't see why you can't live happily at Two Creeks and leave Millicent and me happily here. I do sometimes wonder why we keep such a big house on. It's really a white elephant in these times. . . ."

"*Mother!*" said Millicent, exasperated.

"Yes, dear," Mrs Reddin said, "I know how you feel. But you see, it's going to be all right with Carey after all. I know you wanted Oliver to marry Jane because Jane absolutely adores this place. I've always rather thought, dear, that Jane wanted it as a kind of setting. We might be better off with Carey after all."

Carey was so surprised at this revealing conversation she could think of nothing to say. She was sure Oliver was not in the least likely to consult her about any plans he might have in view that concerned the house or his mother and Millicent.

She patted Mrs. Reddin's hand.

"Please don't worry," she said. "I would never do anything that would make you unhappy. You see, that would make Oliver unhappy, too."

61

She leaned forward and kissed Mrs. Reddin on the forehead. Millicent showed no signs of wanting to be kissed so Carey looked at her, smiled, and said:

"Good-bye, Millicent. I hope you will come to Two Creeks before long."

"Yes, I'll have to do that," said Millicent in a voice heavy with duty. "All the curtains should be taken down before Christmas. And the pantry and store gone through. I expect to be there quite a week when I do come. There is always so much that has to be done at Two Creeks."

Carey as she went out of the door and down the staircase thought about those words of Millicent's. When Millicent came to Two Creeks she expected to supervise the annual cleaning and renovating. That might be very hard to avert. Carey didn't know much about Oliver's attitudes but of this one she was certain. He had asked Carey could she manage Millicent on the very day he had said they should get married.

They drove out west along the great highway into the flat treeless country where the paddocks were yellow with dandelions, then into undulating country with the mountains in the distance.

Oliver drove at a great speed. The big car under them was so beautifully sprung it seemed as if they drove through the air instead of on the ground.

His manner relaxed a great deal now. He spoke quite often about the properties they passed. Carey could see that he had only one love, one real interest in life. It was what went on on the land. He had forgotten she was his wife, or his problem. She was simply someone to sit there in silence and listen while he made comments on the state of the pastures or crops ; the fitness or otherwise of the stock.

CHAPTER SEVEN

Night had fallen when they turned into the home paddock of Two Creeks. Even in the starlight the white painted cross pieces of the fence looked so well care for . . . so *rich* . . . that Carey felt a swelling of pride in her heart.

For the first time she realised she had not only come home, she had come to *her* home. Two Creeks was hers, too. Something to cherish and be proud of.

"Oh, I'm so glad we came home to-day," she said, as the car pulled up in the gravel way below the veranda steps. "This is much nicer than staying in Melbourne."

Oliver had shut off the engine and was opening his door when she spoke.

"You like the country better than the city?" he asked.

"Of course," Carey said. There was a note of happiness in her voice. "I'm a country girl, aren't I?"

Oliver got out and walked round the car to open the door for her. She got out of the car and stood looking out between the trees to where the paddocks were dark pools of distance between the white painted fences. She seemed unaware that he was standing silently beside her.

"Oh, the beautiful smell of it! And I've always taken for granted that tremendous span of sky. I've only had bits of it in Melbourne. But now . . ."

She realised she was talking to herself. Oliver had stood silent by the car a moment and then had begun to take the cases from the boot of the car. He paid no attention to Carey's ecstasies.

A little crestfallen she followed him up the steps across the veranda to the front door. The veranda light was suddenly switched on and the door opened. Hannah stood there in her night attire, a dressing-gown held bunched around her.

"Goodness me, Mr. Oliver, what a fright you gave us. Saw your headlights shining right in my rom, I did, as you came up the drive. Come in, sir, and Miss Carey, too. Why ever didn't you let us know?"

"Miss Carey is now my wife," said Oliver, taking Carey's arm and ushering her in through the door past the bewildered Hannah. "And I didn't let you know because I didn't know I was coming until I got here."

Carey inside the hall looked at him in surprise.

"I did have a passing idea we might go on up into the mountains," Oliver said, then turned to Hannah. "Has Cook got something in the refrigerator we might have for supper? Never mind about the rooms. My wife can use the best guest room for the time being. Our immediate need is tea. Bring out the orange pekoe, will you, Hannah. William has retired for the night, I suppose?"

William was the yardman who usually did things like bringing in the suitcases.

"I'm afraid so, Mr. Oliver. I can see the light on down

63

the passage now which means Cook's heard your voice. She'll have the kettle boiling in no time. And there's always something in the pantry . . . you know that, sir."

"Then take my wife up to her room, will you? I'll get the other cases from the car and bring them all in."

Hannah in her surprise had not yet spoken to Carey. She stood now looking at her half in pleasure, half with embarrassment.

"I certainly am sorry, Miss Carey. I'd have had flowers in your room. And I didn't know where Mr. Oliver was to be moved to now he'd got married. . . ."

"Don't worry, Hannah," Carey said. "We're both very tired. All we want is somewhere to sleep. . . ."

She followed Hannah across the hall and up the stairs, along a carpeted passage towards the guest room. Carey had not been in it before and she was now pleasantly surprised at its comfort and size. It wasn't quite as old-fashioned as the other rooms in Two Creeks. The curtains were of heavy chintz that matched the coverings on the chairs and on the two beds The furniture was fairly modern in design and was made of the beautiful Queensland maple.

Hannah, who had picked up Carey's small case, now put it down by the dressing-table and went at once to the two beds. She began methodically to fold back the covers and turn down the sheets and blankets.

"They'll be quite ready for use, Miss Carey," she explained. "We often have visitors coming unexpectedly and this room is always kept ready. The clothes were aired only yesterday. The bathroom is through that door there. Shall I open the window for you, Miss Carey? It's quite warm for the time of the year. . . ."

"Yes, please do. This room looks over the side lawn and the paddocks, doesn't it, Hannah? Oh . . . and Hannah, how is Tony? Is he all right?"

"As all right as that young monkey will ever be. Never a sight of him for the four days Mr. Oliver's been gone to Melbourne to get married." She let her hands drop by her side, and looked at Carey. "Miss Carey . . . I'd like you to know . . ." She faltered and stopped. A minute later Carey had taken her hands and kissed her.

"I know, Hannah. I do know. You love Mr. Oliver and you've served him here and at Cranston for twenty years.

He belongs to you just as much as he ever did. I won't take him away from you. I just want you to take me into your heart along with him. You see . . ."

No, she couldn't tell even faithful Hannah that she wanted to crawl into someone's heart for warmth herself. She would have to win that place over the years.

"Please, I would love that tea, if you think Cook might have it ready soon." Her eyes were bright and Hannah wiped a small tear surreptitiously from her own.

"I'll go and see," said Hannah.

Oliver came into the room with one of Carey's cases. He ignored the two beds with their covers turned down. He put the case beside the first bed and said:

"I think my study is as comfortable as any other place at this hour of the night. When you're ready come down to it, Carey, and we'll have some supper."

He went back to the door. He hesitated a moment as if he might say something more but changing his mind went out into the hall. Carey wondered where he was walking to . . . his own bedroom somewhere else?

Carey never knew how she got through that supper, got through the process of bathing, and got into bed.

To begin with, she was unutterably tired. Looking at Oliver's face as he sat drinking his tea and merely toying with the chicken salad Cook had brought in on a great silver tray like the one Carey had seen in Mrs. Reddin's bedroom that morning, she knew that he too felt that way.

The wedding reception the night before and the long cross country drive this day had taken its toll.

Oliver was preoccupied but as he served Carey with some chicken salad he made an effort at conversation.

"I think we had both better have a good night's sleep. I have to be out early with the horses to-morrow. It will probably take you several days to get over the affairs of the last two days. I suggest you stay in bed to-morrow, Carey. Perhaps in a day or two's time we might talk over the future."

"I would like to see Tony."

"As soon as he knows you are here he'll put in an appearance. Doors aren't any barrier to Tony when he has a mind to go through them. That is one of the first

65

things you might teach him, Carey. Other people's rights to privacy."

"He is very small and very young," Carey said with pity. "If his mother has been dead some years I don't suppose anyone ever told him not to walk in and out of the rooms."

"My dear girl, I've told him often, and more than once with a wallop behind."

"Don't ever wallop him while I'm around, will you, Oliver? I would feel very upset . . ."

"You have a lot of upsets in store for you with young Tony. And there are other things to be concerned about. You will get on all right with Cook and Hannah, I think. . . ."

"Oh yes, I will," Carey said eagerly. "Please don't worry about anything inside the homestead. We'll manage that between us."

"I hope you do. Now if you are finished I think we should both go to bed. I'm going to be very busy in the next few days so I want you to settle in as best you can without me. The only thing I need to be consulted about is ' callers.' There may be some for business, or social reasons later on. The latter will be your affair and the former mine. We can talk about that sometime later. Neighbours will not call for a week or two. That is the custom in this Shire."

He had risen and he spoke as if he wanted to be alone as quickly as possible. Carey knew now that whatever had happened to make him so angry with her when he had come into her room last night had had a lasting effect. He was infinitely more a stranger to her than he had been even before she had gone to Mrs. Cleaver's house.

Carey stood up and went to the door.

"Good night, Oliver," she said.

"Good night, Carey."

As she went across the hall up the stairs towards the "guest room" she could hardly believe this was happening to her. She had hoped, even believed, that being at home at Two Creeks would have had some softening effect. Yet in that half-hour in the study he had grown, minute by minute, more cold and remote.

Oddly enough, as she got into bed, she thought only of how sad it would make Mrs. Cleaver feel.

She fell asleep with the comforting thought that in the

morning she would see Tony: and one day she would invite Mrs. Cleaver to come to Two Creeks.

Oliver sat, his hands resting on the arms of his chair. His eyes were empty because he was not thinking of this room nor of Carey who had just left it. He was following a train of thought that, if he were less tired, he would have banished from his mind.

As Carey had come into the room the peculiar angle of the light bracket on the wall had caused a shaft of light to shine red-gold on Carey's head. For a moment he had thought of the light through the reception room window shining on Jane Newbold's head last night as he stood with her in a niche between the pot-plant stands on the veranda of Cranston.

She had taken his arm with what might have appeared to other people as a sisterly gesture.

"Come, Oliver," she said, laughing, as if she had something amusing to show him. "Come quick, like a dear. Remember the moon flower we brought down from the Territory? It's actually blooming." She smiled at his elderly and not very astute relatives. "It only blooms for an hour, then when the moon wanes it dies," she explained to them. "Please do forgive me taking Oliver away. He must see it."

Oliver went through the french window to the corner where the plants were growing in pots on stands and looked at the white exotic trumpet of the moon flower.

"Very pretty, Jane, but I don't think that is the plant that came down from the Territory. Millicent has quite a number of them. I think she arranged the steam pipes below the veranda specially to get a few flowers in bloom just now."

"I wanted you to see it because I wanted to be alone with you," Jane said at once.

"My dear girl, this is my wedding night. I can't be alone with anyone. . . ."

"I'm glad you said that."

Oliver was surprised at the tone in Jane's voice.

"Why?" He had moved a little as if to encourage her to turn about and return with him to the reception room.

"Because you'll never be alone with—with Car-eey. My shadow will always be there. Between you." She put out both her hands and caught Oliver's arms with them. She held him so tightly he could not have thrown them off without causing a scene.

"I was the first girl . . . the only girl you loved, Oliver. Oh . . . I know I wouldn't have you. You remember that night so long ago? You were dancing with me. I was the belle of the ball. You remember? You have not forgotten. . . ."

"*Jane!*" His voice was low and urgent. "We cannot stand here talking about the past. It is the past. It happened long ago."

With a quick powerful movement he released himself from her hands He caught her wrists in his own hands and held them behind her back. She was powerless there. In a minute he would turn her round so that he could then escape from this prison of creeper-covered wall and moonlight scented flowers and ferns.

He stood over her, leaning over her. She was imprisoned by his arms which held her struggling hands at her back.

"Yes . . . but you haven't forgotten." Suddenly she let the tenseness seep away from her body. She flung her head back. "That is why my shadow will always fall between you. Every time you go near her you will think of something more exotic. You will think of moon flowers and tropic ferns, a night when you and I danced and when I said 'No' in the middle of the second bar of the encore. You turned and walked off the dance floor. You went back to Two Creeks that night. . . ."

"If you have no objection, Jane, I am going to return to the reception room. My absence would be unforgivable. And it may be noticed."

"It has been," Jane said. "I definitely smiled twice at Millicent as we came through the door. Millicent knows you better than you know yourself, Oliver."

He had already released her hands. He walked to the door. He stood aside.

"Will you go in first, Jane?"

"No, I shan't go in at all. Look what you've done to my wrists . . . you beast."

"Good night, Jane."

She laughed. It was a mocking laugh and it still echoed in Oliver's ears as he went through the door into his own wedding party.

He went to Millicent's side.

"How much longer does this go on, Millicent?" he asked. "Aren't the wedding guests tired yet? I certainly am."

Millicent looked at her brother with curious eyes.

"If Carey likes to change her dress and come in to say good night they'll begin to drift away. But Oliver . . ." She put a detaining hand on his arm. "I want to say something to you. Come into the small drawing-room and we'll have a glass of champagne together."

"I don't think I should leave this room. . . ."

"You have just left it. With Jane. I'm sure your sister is less dangerous, and it is only natural we should have a last glass of goodwill together."

She turned and led the way into the drawing-room.

Oliver pulled the cork of a bottle with its usual " plop." He filled the two glasses with the pale yellow bubbly.

He lifted his glass and looked at Millicent with a strained smile.

"Thank you for arranging the wedding reception," he said. "It was a big job and you've done it magnificently."

"That is what I wanted to speak to you about, Oliver. I did it because I would not have the family let down on a big occasion like this. One had to put the best possible front on your marriage. To marry Carey was a quixotic thing to do, Oliver, and you know it. However, you've done it and I on my part have done my best to put on the best possible front for you. What I wanted to say is this . . . Now that the ceremony is over you have to face up to the fact you are stuck with the results of that same quixotic gesture. You will have to be very careful how you handle Carey. She is a child. Be prepared for tantrums or childish aspirations." Millicent sipped her champagne. "You should have sent Carey packing back to her uncle, and have married Jane. Now I have said it and I promise I will never bring it up or mention it again. I honestly don't think it will last, but I'll do nothing but maintain a silence on that aspect."

"Millicent," said Oliver, looking at his sister with cold controlled anger. "If I were a police magistrate I'd lock you us. You are a menace to other people's happiness."

He turned and walked to the door and held it open for Millicent to precede him. As they went through he saw Jane entering the reception room from the french window on the far side. Jane's eyes met first Millicent's, then Oliver's across the width of the room. She laughed, then shrugged. A minute later she was lost in the guests crowding round the buffet table.

For a painful moment Oliver realised that the only important person in the room who had not noticed that something had happened between the three of them was Carey, smiling serenely in her wedding dress. He went to her side.

"Carey, I think you should go and change now."

She looked up quickly into his face. There was a look of fleeting inquiry in her blue eyes and then one of assent.

"Dear God," he said to himself. "She *is* only a child. What have I done?" Tired shadows were in his eyes and he went to find his mother.

Now, on the following night, Oliver sat in an easy-chair in his study and thought of that succession of scenes at the wedding, and of which Carey was ignorant. It was an effort to banish the picture of Jane coming into the reception room from the veranda . . . and the memory of her earlier words. *My shadow will always be there.* And finally Millicent's . . . *She is a child.*

In the morning Oliver had already gone out on his horse when Carey arose. When she went into the breakfast room adjoining the kitchen Hannah was waiting for her.

"Mr. Oliver said you would be very tired and to leave you to sleep. We didn't think you would be up so early, Miss Carey."

"Seven o'clock?" said Carey. "Goodness, that's late for me really, and I'm dying for my breakfast. Do you think I could have at least two cups of tea to begin with, Hannah?"

"You shall have a whole potful. And will you sit there at the side, Miss Carey. Mr. Oliver always has his breakfast here before he goes out, and he's sat at the window end of the table as long as I can remember."

Hannah looked at the table to make sure everything was right.

"There's a parcel of worry waiting for you out on the back veranda. We've had to keep it locked out like the two cats, the galah and the dog. Otherwise you'd have got no rest. . . ."

"Tony?" cried Carey.

70

Hannah nodded her head resignedly.

"Thank goodness you've come home to look after that one," she said. "Drives me and Cook mad with his wandering in an' out the house, in an' out Mr. Oliver's rooms."

"Hannah dear, just keep my breakfast one minute longer. I want to get Tony . . ."

Carey ran down the side passage and out on to the veranda.

"Tony!" she called. "Tony!"

Dan, one of Oliver's kelpie dogs, pricked his ears. He got up and walked along the veranda to a wooden partition that cut off the corner part of the veranda to make a store house for veranda brooms, tools and odds and ends. He looked at the crack under the door, then back at Carey. He whined softly through his nose.

Along the shelves of the storeroom stood empty plant pots. A pile of old rugs were in one corner and from under this pile obtruded a small boy's leg. It was bare-footed.

Carey, Dan beside her, stooped and lifted off the top pile of rugs.

Tony was lying on his side, his face almost buried in his arm. The only part of his face that was not hidden was one eye. It was watching Carey.

Carey knelt down beside him.

"Tony . . . Tony, darling. Why didn't you come when I called?"

Dan licked the bare leg that had given the hiding-place away.

"Oh, Tony," Carey said, suddenly gathering the small boy up in her arms. Squatting there on the floor she cradled him against her heart.

"You've forgotten me," he mumbled against her shoulder.

There was the sound of heavy footsteps coming across the gravel, then the firm sound of a booted foot stepping up on to the veranda. A few more steps and Oliver Reddin stood in the doorway, looking down at the trio on the floor.

"What are you three doing there?" he asked. "Playing hide-and-seek on the storeroom floor?"

Carey gently put Tony aside and scrambled up.

"Don't let me interrupt you," said Oliver shortly. "I've only come in for my water boots. I've got a couple of sheep bogged near the dam from last night's rain."

71

He reached up and lifted the boots which hung from a nail on the wall high above the shelves.

Tony disentangled himself from the rugs and scrambled up.

"Gee . . . we could go down there," he said, looking at Carey, his sulking forgotten. "You ought to see 'em pulling sheep outa the bogs. Grab 'em by the horns and pull. Nine times outa ten you slip and down you go under the sheep. . . ."

"You stay where you are," said Oliver shortly. "I've too much to do to have a parcel of kids getting under foot in the damn' mud."

He had the boots in his hand and he went to the door. He turned and looked at Carey. They had not uttered a word to one another.

She put out one hand.

"Oliver . . ." she said. "Oliver . . . I'd like to come with you."

He did not look at her.

"Tony and the homestead are your affairs, Carey," he said. "It's better that way. . . . That's why we married, isn't it? Now run along and do your share. I'll go down to the dam and do mine."

Carey felt herself going cold all over.

Run along, tiresome little girl! That is what he meant. Very well! That is what she would do, but not quite in the manner that Oliver Reddin, her *husband*, intended.

"Come, Tony," she said. "Let's go and have some breakfast. Dan, too. Come on, Danny boy. Your master has given you to us."

As she went through the passage door she heard Oliver crunching away across the gravel down towards the home paddock. The coldness that was inside her, she thought, would be there for ever. She would have to get used to living with it.

CHAPTER EIGHT

Carey, with her small round chin set more firmly than usual, went about the business for which, she thought, Oliver had married her.

In the homestead she got on well with Hannah and Cook. She was too wise to interfere with them when she found that the meals prepared and served on Two Creeks had always been to Oliver's liking.

In Wybong she had learned that the children had their schooling through the Education Department's correspondence courses. She wrote to see if she could get the same service for Tony in Victoria. Within a few days he was enrolled and every morning the small boy was put to work in an unused room at the back of the house and which Hannah helped Carey prepare for Tony's use.

"We'll call it Tony's office, Miss Carey," Hannah said. "He'll like that better than 'schoolroom'."

"How wise you are, Hannah," Carey said gratefully. "We can tell him that it's in an office a man begins to learn so that finally he can become a station manager."

"Where's he going to get his station from?" Hannah asked. "Win the pools, or a lottery?"

"I've got a farm," Carey said gravely. "Who knows . . . one day Tony will grow up and he may run that for me. It will be like his own home by then. And it's home that Tony needs more than anything else."

"My, it was an awful pity watching that farm go to wrack and ruin the way it did . . ." said Hannah.

"Yes," said Carey. "But I've got a friend coming down from Wybong who is going to have the fences put in order. That's the first thing to do. When the fences are in order we can begin to stock it. Do you know, Hannah, I'd just love to put some brumby foals there to graze. Do you suppose Tim Wackett would die of heart failure if he saw brumbies running next door to his stud mares?"

"Well, I guess it's what Mr. Oliver says that goes, and truth to tell I've never seen brumbies. Wild horses, aren't they?"

"Mine would be foals from wild horses. But you see, Hannah, there might be a lot of return in just breeding horses for hacks. Everyday hacks I mean, not race-course *prima donnas*."

Hannah shook her head because in the first place she didn't know what a *prima donna* was and in the second place she knew that where Mr. Oliver and Tim Wackett were concerned blood, breeding, pedigree were the hallmarks of what was fit to be reared or grazed on Two Creeks.

However, Miss Carey with her winning ways and that

lovely smiling face might get even Mr. Oliver to agree to wild horses.

Miss Carey seemed to have her heart set on it, just as she had her heart set on this Mr. Martin coming down from Wybong. And Mr. Oliver had given in to that without a word.

Hannah pushed Tony's work table to a place where it could get the light from the window over his left shoulder.

"There now," she said. "All we need is Tony to do some work."

"I'll have to start by wrenching those binoculars from him," said Carey. "Ever since we've stopped him going down to the stables before lunch he's been joining in the fun down there through binoculars."

"I'm that scared he'll drop and break them," said Hannah. "Cost a fortune, that pair did. Mr. Oliver uses 'em to see what's going on in the far paddocks."

"Do you believe in bribery and corruption, Hannah?" asked Carey as she slit the envelopes containing the first week's work from the Correspondence Class.

"Now just what do you mean by that, Miss Carey?"

"We could begin our first lesson with the promise of a pair of binoculars of his own at the end of the term."

Hannah smiled.

"I always did believe in a piece of barley sugar along with the medicine," she said.

Oliver had been quite right when he said Tony had brains. Carey was astonished at how quickly the boy picked up the first principles of his work. Carey had to ask Oliver if she could send for books of all kinds to keep Tony occupied. She was determined that Tony would do three hours' work a day.

"Send for whatever you want," Oliver said. "I'm glad to see you've got the little tyke to work. What is the charm, Carey?"

"His own horse to be ridden, and taken care of, every afternoon," Carey said. "And he's going to break it in himself."

"His own *what*?" said Oliver. "There's not a four-legged animal on this place that's not worth a fortune. Blood stock . . . even the cattle and sheep. Tony's not touching any of it."

"No, I thought not," Carey said quietly. "You see, I've
74

written to Harry Martin and asked him to bring a couple, or three, young brumby foals with him. Of course they'll be partially broken in but they'll still have enough of mountain memory to make them pretty lively."

" You're having *what* brought to Two Creeks? *Brumbies?* Do you know, Carey, this station has the finest reputation in the country for its stock? One brumby on the place would put a question mark against our integrity as stud masters."

" We'll keep them on my farm," Carey said gently. " Tony and I've mended the fences on the little stabling paddock by the cottage on my farm. I think that will keep them in."

Oliver put down his knife and fork and stared at Carey.

" You and Tony have been mending fences?" he said, underlining every word as if he did not believe one of them.

" Yes," said Carey, looking up in surprise. " I've mended fences before. Of course I've always had to get someone . . . Harry generally . . . to pull the wire from the straining posts. But Tony and I managed, until Harry goes over it for us."

" You are my wife," Oliver said with a touch of anger. " If my wife keeps brumbies on a property next to mine it will raise questions in some people's minds. You had better wire Mr. Martin to lose those animals on the way down here."

Carey was silent and she went on with her meal.

" Do you hear me, Carey?" Oliver said. " You are my wife. . . ."

Carey lifted her eyes to meet his.

" That side of it doesn't matter very much, does it?" she asked quietly. " The important thing is to educate Tony, fix up my farm, and give me a home meantime. I expect people will know about us, Oliver. It's uncanny how people know things about one another. In Wybong . . ."

" Will you please cease to refer to Wybong. If I wanted to emulate the manners and ways of Wybong I would go and live there. As it is, I own a station breeding, amongst other things, pedigreed horses. There will be no suspicion of poor stock being anywhere in my neighbourhood."

" People who have bought from you trust you, Oliver. They wouldn't think you would be foolish enough to adulterate your blood stock."

Oliver had finished his meal. Hannah came in to serve the dessert but Oliver declined it.

" Excuse me, Carey," he said, rising. " I'll see you in

the study later." He went out of the room, leaving Carey to do her best to avoid Hannah's eyes.

"Perhaps you had better bring the coffee to the study, Hannah," Carey said quietly. "I'm afraid Mr. Oliver does not like my brumbies."

"I thought not, miss. I thought not. It's a pity since you've set your heart on it."

A little later Carey went to the study. Oliver stood up as she came in. Sitting alone in the dining-room, making pretence at eating the apricots and ice-cream, she had been having an inner struggle. She didn't want to give in to Oliver. Why, she asked herself, did he have to have his own way about everything?

Oliver stood up when she came in and waited until she had seated herself by the table on which Hannah had put the coffee.

As she lifted the coffee-pot and began to pour she knew she would give in to him. All the same it brought a lump of disappointment to her throat.

It was the coming into the study that had done it. That . . . and seeing him sitting there behind his desk looking so exactly as he had looked the day Uncle Tam had brought her to Two Creeks.

Moreover, to-night there was something tired about his shoulders that had not been there when he came into dinner. Maybe it was a mental effort and a worry to him to have herself and Tony on his mind.

He came round the desk and took his coffee from her hand.

"Very well, Oliver," she said quietly. "I could wire Harry Martin at Albury. I'll tell him to sell . . . or give away . . . the brumbies."

Oliver was stirring his coffee as he went back to his chair. She watched his back as he walked away. It was a broad back with powerful shoulders. His clothes always fitted him beautifully.

"I'm glad you've got some sense about that, Carey," he said as he sat down. He sipped his coffee, frowning. Then he looked up. His eyes were that clear impersonal grey. Carey had never seen them warm with affection . . . or love. Perhaps if she saw him with the horses he loved they would be different.

"I will stock your farm myself," he said. "That is, I will give you and Tony two or three horses, and later

76

when the fences round the boundary are in order I'll put some young Jerseys in down on the creek flats. That is some of the best dairy stock land in the country."

Carey was silent a minute.

"Thank you, Oliver," she said at length. "Of course that will be debited against my farm, won't it?"

"No," he said shortly. "I'm giving them to you. I'll see Tim Wackett in the morning. You may tell Tony he can come down and choose his own mount . . . from what Tim will agree to part with. I'll choose a mount for you myself."

Carey did not know what to say. He was being kind, even generous, yet she would have loved to graze her own mountain brumbies.

"Thank you," she said and sipped her coffee.

"This man Harry Martin? You have known him a long time?"

"Oh, yes. He is my oldest friend."

"You understand there has to be some kind of guarantee about any man who works on or near Two Creeks. Potential racers are tried out on my tracks and I don't want any early morning stop-watches on them."

Carey put down her cup. She could see her own hand trembling. She would have staked her life on Harry Martin's integrity and Oliver's cold business-like words were like sharp needles in her heart.

"If you don't mind, Oliver, I will leave you now," she said rising. "I have one or two things I want to do before I go to bed."

She walked over to the desk and picked up Oliver's empty cup and saucer. She would not raise her eyes to meet his, he might see how angry and hurt she was. She took the cup and saucer and put them on the tray, then lifted the tray and walked towards the door. He stood up with the punctilious kind of automatic courtesy he always showed when she entered or left a room.

"Good night, Carey," he said. She turned, the small coffee-tray balanced on her right hand.

"Good night, Oliver."

She went out across the hall and down the passage to the kitchen.

Some days later Tony was breathing hard as he copied out his spelling in good round script into his dictation book.

77

"Silly words!" he said aloud. "I can spell them all, anyway."

He turned round so that he could see Carey through the window. She was sitting on a chair, leaning her elbows on the veranda railings, looking through the binoculars.

Carey was often sitting that way these days. It was all right for her to say, "Look out you don't drop them, Tony!" She liked looking through the binoculars just as much herself.

He pushed up the window a few inches.

"What are you looking at, Carey?" he asked. "You don't have to do lessons. Why don't you go down to the track yourself?"

Carey did not take her eye away from the glass.

"Yes. I have to do lessons. I have to call your words to you, and show you the things you don't understand. Besides, I'd feel mean going down there leaving you behind."

"Gee . . . you got a kind heart, haven't you!" said Tony derisively.

"Mm. That's just what I have got. There's a big car coming up the main drive. You ought to see it, Tony. Must be a Jaguar or a Bentley by the way it's shaped."

Tony pushed the window wide open and scrambled over the ledge.

"Gee . . . let's have a look, Carey. Be a sport."

Carey moved over and let Tony take the binoculars and put his eye to the glass.

"Wow . . . what a beauty! Say, I've seen that car before. I think it's been here before. Maybe it's one of the racing men who spells his horses on Two Creeks."

"My turn," said Carey.

Tony handed the glass to her.

"There aren't any horses in the show paddock," she said. "But Tim Wackett's just gone inside the saddling room. Ah . . . there's Oliver come out now. He's standing down by the gate. I think he's going to open it for the big car."

"Half the time you look through those things you're looking at what Mr. Oliver's doing, aren't you, Carey? Why don't you go down there with him. If I was married to him, I wouldn't be stuck up here all day. I'd go out with him every day."

"Be quiet, Tony. I'm busy. Go and do your work like

a good boy. As soon as you're finished we'll go down."

Tony turned disconsolately to the window. As he climbed through he offered a parting shot.

"You're different now you're married. You used to like playing and climbing up the creek gully. Now you just like sitting there watching Mr. Oliver. Don't you see enough of him when he comes in at night?"

"I'm not watching Oliver," said Carey. "I'm watching everything. There's sheep all round the dam and over on Cone Hill I can see the cattle moving in a string. And the big car has stopped. Somebody's getting out of it. Why . . . it's a woman!"

"Yes . . ." said Tony. "Lots of women come to buy their horses off Mr. Oliver, too. My dad used to say his good looks sold as many horses as his pedigree book did."

"Get on with your work, Tony."

Carey's voice was quiet. Tony thought it was because she was getting mad at him now. Actually it was because the woman who got out of the big shining green and black car had red hair. And it was Jane Newbold. She was leaning against the front mudguard of her car, looking up at Oliver, and talking to him.

She was smoking a cigarette and Carey could see by her nonchalant attitude that she was enjoying it. Oliver had taken off his broad-brimmed hat and hung it on a fence post. He stood with arms folded, his feet set apart, and looked at Jane.

With a sigh Carey put the binoculars back in their case and hung them on their peg on the veranda wall. She went inside to the kitchen.

"There's a big car down at the stables gate, Cook," Carey said. "We might be having a visitor for lunch, though I expect Mr. Oliver will ring through from the stables if we do. Have we got something extra special?"

"How about some crayfish tails . . . done with a French salad? Mr. Oliver had some flown over from the West Australian coast and they're still in the deep freeze."

"Couldn't we have some southdown lamb and salad, Cook? I mean, if the visitor doesn't come up we'd be wasting the crayfish, wouldn't we?"

"There's something in that. Mr. Oliver gives lunch down at Tim Wackett's lunch room to visitors that come on business."

Carey didn't have the heart to confess to Cook that this particular visitor wouldn't be coming on business. At least not the kind of business that interested Tim Wackett.

How would she greet Jane?

Would she have to take Jane up to her bedroom to do her hair and make-up?

My goodness, how much would that room give away the life she and Oliver led in the homestead? No, that was one thing she couldn't bear . . . Jane's all-seeing eye and Jane's mocking laugh.

Carey went upstairs and along the passage to her bedroom. Everything in the room was, of course, feminine and belonged to Carey. But then didn't all bedrooms of married people look like that? Maybe she ought to have just something of Oliver's to give it the masculine touch.

Carey crossed the hall to Oliver's room. She hardly ever went there; only to put away Oliver's laundry, in fact. Somehow it seemed very private and inviolable.

What could she take and put in her own room to give that masculine touch?

Her eyes went down to the base of the chest of drawers and there, heels just protruding, stood Oliver's house-shoes. Carey darted across the room, picked up the shoes and put them under the bed that stood nearest the window, their heels just showing. She put her own slippers, which generally were hidden in a cupboard, under her own bed. She went back to Oliver's room, took a shirt from a drawer and brought it back and put it over the back of a chair as if ready for him to don.

" There . . . Jane Newbold," she said. She tossed a lock of hair back from her eyes and went to the dressing-table to readjust her make-up. She must have her hair neat, her lips made up . . . and that was all.

In the mirror of the dressing-table she could see the two beds, her own slippers under one bed and Oliver's house shoes under the other, the shirt over the chair back.

It was a shoddy little deception, but she was going through with it. She would have to go through with it. When the glorious red-headed Jane came up with Oliver she, Carey, could hold her head up like any very truly married wife.

Carey went back to the salad making and then to help Tony over any stumbling blocks with his lessons.

It was Tony who vouchsafed the next news bulletin. He had taken down the binoculars and planted himself in Carey's chair, his elbows on the balustrade, the glasses in his eyes.

"Tim Wackett's got two horses in the saddling paddock, Carey. What you bet those are the two horses for me and you? He told me yesterday Mr. Oliver had picked a brown gelding for you and I'm to have a grey one he can't sell for a decent price because he won't jump and he shies at motor-cars."

"Oh . . ." said Carey, wishing that her voice wouldn't sound strained in her own ears. "Are you sure they're the ones? I mean if the grey one shies at motor-cars, it would be playing up with that big car down by the gate, wouldn't it?"

"The car's not there now. It's gone," said Tony. "Mr. Oliver's gone, too. Maybe he's gone over the hills to look at the cattle. Or maybe he's taken the lady to look at something out in the horse paddock."

"Yes . . . maybe," said Carey. "Tony dear, put those binoculars up now, will you? If Oliver comes in and catches you with them he'll be mad. You know that."

"Aw . . . he won't come in. He doesn't ever come up for lunch, Carey."

"All the same put them up, will you, Tony. Maybe this afternoon after lunch we'll go down and look at those horses."

"Why can't we go now? There's time, isn't there?"

"No . . . there's not time. Besides, if they are for us I think it would be polite to wait for Oliver to give them to us . . . ceremoniously, if you know what I mean."

"He'll forget," said Tony peevishly as he hung up the glasses. "He forgets all about you and me."

Yes, thought Carey sadly, I sometimes think that myself.

Lunch-time came and went and there was no sign of Oliver or his visitor.

"Must have been just another buyer," Cook said to Carey. "You don't want to take notice of the comings and goings down there at the stables, Miss Carey. Half the people what calls there Mr. Oliver wouldn't invite up to the homestead anyway."

Half-way through the afternoon the telephone went at long last. Carey tried not to fly to it.

It wasn't Oliver, it was Millicent on a long distance call from Melbourne. She was coming out to Two Creeks and would get there late to-morrow afternoon. Was there anything Carey or Oliver wanted brought out from Melbourne?

"Yes please, Millicent," Carey said. "Would you call in at the big bookshop on the corner of Little Collins Street and collect the order for Tony. It would save waiting for the delivery. Are you bringing Mrs. Reddin?"

No, Mrs. Reddin was spending some days on the south coast with a cousin. Hence Millicent's freedom. She said "freedom" as if it was something of which Mrs. Reddin had deprived her by continuing to exist into elderly infirmity. Carey privately thought it was Mrs. Reddin who would be enjoying freedom.

She put back the telephone receiver on its cradle. Now, she thought, will begin the real test of my wifehood. Do I . . . or do I not . . . manage Millicent.

And there had not been a word about "dear Jane."

Carey was too kind to think that Millicent and Jane might have wangled it to meet at Two Creeks but she expected it might happen.

The important question now was . . . did she tell Cook to prepare something special for dinner, in case Oliver brought Jane in then? Where, she wondered, would they have gone together? Somewhere in the car, of course, because the car had gone from the drive near the stables. She decided against special preparation. If Oliver did not announce Jane's presence he wouldn't expect dinner to be any different from usual.

Carey, now with the excuse of Millicent's imminent arrival, was able to go about the business of dusting and preparing the second guest room. If Jane came up she could go in there after all.

But Carey forgot to return Oliver's house-shoes and shirt to their rightful places.

Nightfall came and Carey, brushing her hair by her open window, heard Oliver's horse coming up the rise to the home stable. There was no accompanying hum of a motor-car. Carey's spirits rose. Perhaps Jane had gone away . . . wasn't coming after all. Dear God, she would be thankful for that. She was not very afraid of Millicent . . . but she was very afraid of Jane. And very, very afraid of the combination of the two of them.

She heard Oliver coming into the house, and presently

the sounds of his going from his room to the bathroom. There was the faint buzz of his electric shaver, then the sound of water pouring from the shower.

Carey went downstairs and into the dining-room and sat down in a chair by the window. Oliver had brought the mail in and put it in a pile on the end of the long dining-table. Carey took her pile of letters. They were all from Wybong including one from Uncle Tam.

They were all full of love and kindness and good wishes for her marriage.

"Goodness, I didn't know so many people were interested in me," she thought. She was astonished to read their testimony to the love they felt for her. "Goodness!" she kept saying. "Imagine them writing to *me*. . . ."

For two weeks now these letters had been pouring into Two Creeks and the only thing Carey could think of saying to express her astonishment that there was so much feeling for her in the world was . . . "*Goodness!*"

When Oliver came into the dining-room she had just finished reading the last one and she put it with the others in her pocket.

For some reason Oliver had put on a dark suit to-night. In the shaded light from the wall brackets it made him look remote and shadowy but very distinguished. His hair was shining and brushed down hard against his head, showing what a very well-shaped head he had. The edges of his teeth shone in his sun-bronzed face.

"Are we ready for dinner?" he asked. "I see you have taken your mail."

"Yes, thank you," said Carey. "I'll tell Hannah . . ."

"It's all right. I will." He went to the door again. "We're ready, Hannah, when you are. And you might bring in a bottle of Sauterne. I think there's one in the fridge."

He came back to the dining-room table and held Carey's chair while she sat down. He then went to his own place, sat down and took his napkin from its ring.

"Tony bedded down for the night?" he asked.

"Yes. Mrs. Wackett still prefers him to sleep there, but I would like him to come up to the homestead. Do you think we could turn that back box-room into a room for Tony, Oliver?"

Oliver frowned.

"Time enough when we see how he settles down to lessons

and some kind of orderly routine. We can't begin a thing we may not want to go on with. It's easy enough to bring him up here, but would be hard to change our minds and send him packing."

Carey spread her napkin delicately on her lap.

"I don't think I would ever send Tony packing," she said.

"No, but I would," said Oliver. "If he doesn't measure up. Oh, thank you, Hannah. Just leave the bottle on the tray. We'll have it after our soup."

Hannah had brought in the bottle of white wine on a silver tray and she now left it on the table near Oliver's left hand.

"Any news of the homestead to-day, Hannah?" he asked.

"No, Mr. Oliver. Only that Miss Millicent's coming to-morrow. I expect Miss Carey's told you about that."

"I haven't had time yet," said Carey. She looked at Oliver. "Millicent rang up from Melbourne this afternoon. . . ."

Oliver looked thoughtful. Then the edge of a sardonic smile showed on his lips.

"We'd better drink to that," he said. "I was wondering what kind of an excuse I could find for having a bottle of Sauterne."

"I wondered if you had a special reason. Has something pleasant or unusual happened, Oliver?"

"No. I just felt like Sauterne to-night."

He fell silent as Hannah put the soup before them.

He hadn't mentioned Jane. In a minute he would tell her, of course, that Jane had been on Two Creeks. Perhaps she had only called in, or brought a message. In a minute Oliver would mention it.

The soup was finished. Oliver carved the roast beef and they ate it in comparative silence. While waiting for it they had drunk their wine in the same silence. With the dessert Carey spoke.

"It might be nice having Millicent. We don't have many visitors to the homestead, do we?"

The words were no sooner out of her mouth than she felt guilty of probing. Deep in her heart she knew she was giving Oliver a lead to tell her Jane had called to-day. She didn't want to hear about Jane, only that Jane's presence was not a cause for reticence on Oliver's part.

84

"If the visit passes with you managing Millicent and not Millicent managing you, it might be a good idea," Oliver said. He looked at Carey thoughtfully. "I am afraid you have a family now, Carey. You might as well get to know the members of it properly."

Carey thought of the letters in her pocket and the others in the bottom of her glove drawer. She had a family . . . a very big one . . . but she could not tell Oliver about it because the subject of Wybong was forbidden. And he, of course, would never understand how a girl of eighteen could have a whole town full of family, not one of which, except Uncle Tam, was related by blood ties.

Carey began to think now that he was not going to tell her of his visitor at all. As the meal progressed her spirits sank lower and it was hard for her to keep smiling as if this was just an ordinary day. Hannah had said that Carey always smiled. So she mustn't stop on the day of Jane's visit.

The meal finished. Oliver stood up.

"I think we'll have coffee in the drawing-room to-night," he said unexpectedly. Then added quickly, as an after-thought, "We might as well practise in readiness for Millicent. Everything is done by the book where Millicent is concerned."

"I'll tell Hannah," Carey said and hurried off in the direction of the kitchen pantry.

Why the Sauterne for dinner? Why Oliver's dark suit and that groomed appearance? Why coffee in the drawing-room? Was he celebrating something, if only just a mood? And what would put him in a mood different to-night from other nights?

"Coffee in the drawing-room, Hannah, if you don't mind," she said. "And would you pour Mr. Oliver's? I'll be back presently."

She went out on to the veranda and stood, her cheek leaning against a veranda post. She closed her eyes to shut out the great vista of limitless starry sky and the endless shadow of the paddocks that stretched away as far as human eye could see in the glorious streaming moonlight.

"If only he'd told me she was here," she thought. "If only he'd told me."

She could not bring herself to go into the drawing-room. She walked the length of the veranda and then down the

85

steps and across the lawn. She walked on across the track, across the fallow paddock, towards the wire fence that was the boundary between Two Creeks and her own farm.

At the fence she stood leaning against a post and looking over the waste of bracken-ridden furrows.

" I must have something to live for," she thought. " I must have something to live and work for. It will be this . . . my farm. When Harry comes it will be different. I know how Harry works. Day by day the fences will be put in order, day by day that bracken will be pushed back and back into the bush. And I'll have Harry to talk to. . . ."

There was a lump in her throat as she saw herself and Harry Martin working, side by side, bringing beauty and order again to that stretch of country. Making the earth to flower again.

She turned and went back to the homestead. The house was a blaze of lights, and even as she went up the steps on to the veranda she could see Hannah's figure hurrying through the hall. Carey went in through the side door. The lights were on in Oliver's study . . . in the passage . . . in the hall . . . in the bathroom. In his bedroom.

" What is the matter, Hannah " she asked. " Is the place on fire "

" No. It's Mr. Oliver's house-shoes. If there's one thing Mr. Oliver can't stand it's my not putting his shoes back in their right place. If I leave them around the floor there's the dickens to pay. But I'm certain they were right there in his room this morning. Where they always are. . . ."

Carey's hand went to her mouth.

" Yes, they were, Hannah . . ." she said. " I—I took them. . . ."

Oliver had gone into his room and changed from his dark suit into an older pair of trousers and a reefer jacket. This, with his house-shoes, was a favourite form of dress when he was going to work late at night in his study. He heard Carey speaking to Hannah in the passage and he came to the door.

" What goes on" he demanded. " Have you found my shoes yet, Hannah."

" Well . . . er . . . no, Mr. Oliver. You see . . ."

" I took them," said Carey. " I can't—I can't quite think where I put them."

"You took them?" said Oliver. "What on earth did you take my shoes for? Where did you have them?"

"Would you go and look on the veranda? Or in that storeroom, Hannah? I might have had them there with Tony."

"With Tony?" demanded Oliver. "What is Tony doing with my possessions? I've said before he is not to come wandering in and out the rooms of the homestead. Specially *my* rooms.'

"It wasn't Tony. It was *me*," said Carey.

"Now you're protecting him, of course."

"No. I was just playing with him. You know . . . 'Big Shoes, Little Shoes ' . . . a game we played when we were children. If you'll just go into your study and wait, Oliver, I'll bring them to you."

She walked away down the passage to her own room. She shut the door behind her so that neither Hannah nor Oliver would see her take the shoes from under that bed, but the door latch did not click to a lock.

She crossed the room and stooped down and picked up the shoes. When she straightened up she knew by the cool draught of air that the door had opened. She turned round. Oliver was standing there.

There was a silence between them for a moment, then Oliver came into the room, shutting the door behind him. This time the lock clicked.

He walked across the thick pile of carpet and took the shoes out of Carey's hand. His eyes had a probing question in them.

"Why did you take them, Carey?" he asked.

She looked up at him. For a minute she had an overwhelming temptation to tell him, but she remembered suddenly that amongst other admonitions Oliver had told her to "grow up." It was the "tiresome little girl" theme all over again. And of course she couldn't tell him the truth about her fear of Jane's searching eye and mocking smile.

She pulled herself together. She must stand between him and that chair where his shirt was hung.

"I might be going to make you a pair of socks," she said with a laugh. "Who knows? I'll have to do something in the winter evenings. Now you have the shoes you could change into them . . . and . . . well . . . and be able to get on with your work, Oliver."

Some change seemed to go through Oliver. He drew in his breath.

"You are still afraid of me, Carey, aren't you?" His grey eyes looked deep into her blue eyes.

Carey went over to her dressing-table. She moved a silver trinket tray with one finger.

"Any girl would be afraid of a strange man in her room," she said at length and a little sadly. "And you are strange to me, Oliver. I do not understand you. And you do not understand me."

"Yes, I do understand you, Carey," he said, still standing three yards away. "You're a child who refuses to grow up."

Carey turned round.

"How do you know that I am only a child, Oliver?"

He frowned.

"What do you mean?"

Again the truth was on the tip of her tongue . . . *Why don't you tell me who comes and goes on Two Creeks? Why must I remain in ignorance of Jane's visit? And why don't you treat me as your wife? Your real true and loving wife?*

"Would you please go, Oliver," she said gravely. "I want my room to myself."

It was very seldom there was no smile on Carey's face. It was markedly absent now. Oliver noticed the difference. It was his presence that caused that difference.

"Very well, Carey." He went to the door and opened it. "If you care to come down to the stables in the morning I'll give you and Tony a couple of horses to play with." There was an edge of bitterness in his voice as he emphasised the word "play."

He was gone, and the door closed firmly behind him.

Carey drew in a quavering breath.

"So ends a not-so-perfect day," she thought. She went to her bed and sat down on it. As she moved she heard the rustle of the letters in her pocket. She took them out, and one by one looked at them. She lay back on her pillow holding the letters; and wrote letters in her mind. They were to everyone who loved her in Wybong.

An hour later Oliver, irritated by a restlessness that would not let him work, came to her dor. It was the absence of Carey's smile that had stung him most. He had a cup of tea which he had made in the pantry. Carey was lying on her pillow, the letters still in her hand. Her lashes lay like twin fringes on her cheeks. On her pillow under her cheek was a shirt. His shirt.

Oliver put the tea cup on the table and stood looking down at Carey. Then he bent over her and lifted her feet so they lay comfortably on the bed, and drew the shirt from under her head. He slipped off her shoes. With the movement Carey drew in a sigh that was half a sob as if in her sleep she was weeping. The letters dropped from her hand.

Oliver stooped and picked them up from the floor. A loose leaf lay face down and as Oliver picked it up he turned it over. It contained the last two lines of a letter.

So Carey love, I'll be with you Friday. And a saddle bag full of nice surprises I've got for you.
Love,
Ever Yours,
Harry

Oliver folded the sheet and put it in its envelope. He pushed all the letters under Carey's pillow. He took a light rug from the window-seat and spread it over her.

Carey sighed and turned over. Oliver stood looking down at her. He brushed his hand over his own forehead, and then turned, picked up the unwanted tea cup and the crumpled shirt and as he went out of the room he turned off the light.

CHAPTER NINE

Millicent's arrival was in capital letters. She swung her big car up the drive and braked with deliberate importance. She got out of the car and shut the door in a manner that announced her arrival with a full stop.

The rouseabout appeared round a corner before Millicent had taken one step, and Hannah stood in the open door patting down her white apron.

Carey was at the drawing-room window and watched Millicent address the rouseabout on the subject of her luggage and then look up the steps towards the open door and Hannah.

Beyond Millicent and her car the sun was disappearing over the western ledge of the world. Everything in the paddocks was still, and watchful. Nothing moved or sounded except Millicent's steps as she crossed the short gravel space and mounted the stone steps of Two Creeks.

Then her voice could be heard and a sort of minor well-bred commotion broke the evening peace.

"Oh, there you are, Hannah! See that William takes my case up to my usual room, will you? And William . . . kindly don't scratch the surface of the case. Hannah . . . is my brother in from the run yet? And I suppose my sister-in-law is somewhere about?"

Sister-in-law! Good heavens, Carey thought, I hadn't realised I was anything as related as that.

She went to the drawing-room door as Millicent entered the hall.

Did she kiss, or shake hands?

Millicent settled that by saying: "Oh, hallo. There you are!" then hunting in her handbag for her keys to give to Hannah.

"Just put everything in the usual place," she said to Hannah and then turned to Carey. "I'm dying for a cup of tea. Is Oliver in yet?"

"Do come in, Millicent," Carey said, standing aside so that Millicent could enter the drawing-room. "I arranged for some tea to be ready for you; and no . . . Oliver is not in yet."

Millicent stood quite still in the middle of the big, charming room and looked around.

"You haven't altered anything. Well, thank goodness for that." She sat down in a button-backed arm-chair. "You do, of course, realise that this room is original period? I mean the room is furnished as it originally was furnished by our great-grandparents. Not a single thing in it is imported or has been added."

"Yes, I do know," Carey interrupted her gently. "I wouldn't dream of altering anything in a room as unusual and unique as this room, Millicent. If I want to have any ideas of my own I'll have them in the new part of the home-stead."

"Well, don't do anything without consulting Oliver. And of course he will refer anything like that to me . . . just as a precaution, of course."

Carey laughed. It was a clear friendly tinkling laugh.

"Any alterations are a long, long way away," she said. "I shouldn't get anxious about them just now."

"I was really more concerned with the curtains and window fixtures. I think we'd better begin with the curtains in here, in the small sitting-room, and Oliver's study. There are alternative curtains to put up while these go to the dry-cleaning people."

"I'm very glad to see you, Millicent," Carey said. "You haven't give me an opportunity to say so yet. Do you think I'm looking well?"

Millicent stopped in mid flight and looked across the room at Carey.

"Well, yes. As a matter of fact, you do look well. I'm very glad to see you are looking well, Carey."

"And I suppose you are wondering if Oliver looks well? He does, you know. Very well."

"I was not wondering that at all, Carey. The Reddins are a strong and healthy family and they always look well. It never ocurs to me to wonder in any way about Oliver's health. Oh, here's Hannah with the tea. Put it here on this table will you, Hannah? I can pour without getting up."

Hannah stood in the middle of the room with the tea-tray in her hands. She looked at Carey. Carey smiled.

"I'll save you the trouble of pouring, Millicent," she said, getting up. "Put it here, Hannah, will you? I'm sure Millicent . . . after that long drive . . . will be relieved not to have any chores for a day or two."

Hannah put the tea-tray on the table Carey indicated, and as she went out Carey hurried on with what she was saying, not allowing Millicent to assert her authority over the matter of who poured out the tea at Two Creeks.

"You have such a lot to do in Melbourne, Millicent. And all your committee work, too. I think you're really wonderful the amount you cram into your life. And I'll always be grateful for the magnificent and effortless way you ran that wedding."

She was pouring the tea as she spoke and she now carried the cup and saucer to Millicent and then placed the milk and sugar bracket on the table beside her.

"Please do have a little rest while you are here. I would so like it to be something of a holiday for you."

"Oh . . . if you only knew how I need a holiday!" said Millicent, putting her tea on the table. "You've no idea what a strain it is keeping up a position in Melbourne. Every kind of charity organisation under the sun wants one to do

91

committee work. Of course I always give my time first to the Red Cross and the military hospitals. Then there's Mother. . . ."

" I hope Mother . . ." Carey blushed and corrected herself. " I hope Mrs. Reddin will come and stay for some time on Two Creeks. It would give you both a holiday."

" My dear child, you do not know what managing Mother is like. If I didn't keep a weather eye on her the whole time she would have the Reddin family under censure throughout Australia." She looked at Carey. " When one is old, you know, it is very easy to let one's standards slip. I mean take the easy way out. So many people have, you know. Serving dinner in a buffet style. Can you imagine it? I simply won't permit it at Cranston . . . or Two Creeks either for that matter. If someone is worthy of being asked to dinner . . . then dinner should be served properly."

Carey had a fleeting vision of herself putting a huge meal on the table in the centre room on Uncle Tam's grazing block and calling to the stockmen, " Come and get it!" and the stockmen crying, " Whacko, it's on!"

When one·didn't have servants what else was there to do?

Also she wondered how to go about stopping Millicent calling her " my dear child." She wondered why neither Oliver nor Millicent would let her be an adult.

" And that reminds me," said Millicent. " Yes, please, I will have another cup of tea. Yes, that reminds me . . . Jane Newbold will be here at the end of the week. I expect she will stay a few days. She will have the front guest room as usual. I was wondering if we had better leave the present curtains there for the time being."

Carey tried very hard not to blush and not to let her voice shake.

" That is my room now," she said as matter-of-factly as possible. " I think I would like to refurnish the big bedroom on the other side of the pasage before I . . . we . . . use it."

That " we " only just crept out and Carey found her fingers pressing down the pleats at the side of her dress with a kind of nervous desperation. Fortunately Millicent was concentrating more on the audacity of returning a Two Creeks room than on Carey's faltering " we."

" My dear child . . ." she began.

" Do you think the room next to yours would be nice for Jane?" Carey asked, wondering why her brain was still functioning when her nervous system was going into a top spin. "It's such a charming room. And you know, Millicent, those blue curtains and the blue carpet would somehow just set off Jane's red hair. Jane is such an awfully effective kind of person, isn't she?"

"I'm glad you admire her," Millicent said, mollified. "So you ought to do, of course. Her looks . . . her money . . . her position! Yes, Jane has everything!"

Yes, everything, thought Carey soberly. But why didn't Oliver marry *her*?

Her mind winced away from the thought because she suddenly could see exactly why Millicent called her "my dear child" and Oliver treated her as one. Beside Jane she would look slight and insignificant. And she didn't have money, or position.

Again her thoughts flew back to Wybong.

But she had love. She was sure she had love in Wybong.

"It will be nice for you and Oliver having an old friend staying next week-end," Carey said. "Because I have one, too. Harry Martin is coming down from Wybong and he should be here by Friday."

Millicent frowned.

"Harry Martin?" she asked, puzzled. "Oh, you mean the man who's going to do the fencing on your farm. Well, that will be nice for you. Being a fencer he will, of course, stay down at the quarters."

"He is my friend and Uncle Tam's friend. Besides, he's not a fencer, Millicent. He's a contractor and at Wybong he is a very important man."

Millicent had finished her tea and she now stood up.

"My dear child . . . Wybong is not even on the pastoral map and life there would be very primitive compared with the old-established parts of Victoria. I think I'll go upstairs now and have a bath before dinner." She had reached the door. "Oh, by the way, Jane is up at Mount Macedon for a few days' rest. She thought of calling in on her way up to let you know she'd be staying this week-end. I suppose she didn't have time."

"She may have seen Oliver somewhere out on the property," Carey said, turning away to hide her face as she tried to evade the implications in the fact that Jane *had* called in, *had* seen Oliver, and Oliver had not told her, Carey, the portent of that fleeting visit.

And as for Wybong being primitive! She wished Millicent could see Cartheroo station with its own aeroplane, its concrete swimming-pool, its silent swivelling fans in every room, its refrigeration plant, its *everything*. But how did anyone tell Millicent anything? It would be like flatly contradicting her. And Carey could never bring herself to do that to anyone.

Millicent's thoughts were still on Jane.

"Oliver didn't mention anything to you?" she asked, one inquiring eyebrow raised.

Carey now had to face the other.

"No," she said quietly. "Oliver doesn't mention very much to me. He is very busy, and you see . . . I have Tony."

Millicent was silent a minute.

"Oh," she said. "So it is like that, is it?"

"Yes," said Carey calmly. "It is like that."

Across the room they looked at one another in silence.

"Well," said Millicent, suddenly moving into action again, "I must have my bath. And yes, I quite agree about Jane and the room with the blue curtains. After all she will only need one bed. And there are two in the other room, aren't there?"

"Yes," said Carey.

Somewhere in the house a door closed and then there were heavy firm footsteps approaching down the cross passage.

"That is Oliver now. I will leave you to meet him by yourself, Millicent. I'll take this tray to the kitchen and see—see to Tony."

On Tony's name her voice actually trembled. Someone at Two Creeks to love, by whom to be loved. Yes, she must see to Tony at once. Except that she had to pass Oliver in the hall she would have fled.

As usual the sight of his tall strong figure and his face browned and just a little dusty from his day on the run made her conscious of his physical presence.

"Millicent is here," she said. "She has just gone down to your study, Oliver."

Oliver was hanging his hat on the hat rack in the side passage. He did not look at Carey.

"I saw the car come up about half an hour ago. I expect we'll be a little late for dinner. You might tell Cook, Carey."

"Yes, I will do that," said Carey and went on down the main hall with the tray.

How silly can some people be, she asked herself. Even

94

a strong-minded man like Oliver? Why did he marry me and not Jane Newbold? Was it kindness or just charity, because if it was charity he has picked the wrong client.

Carey hadn't a great many years behind her but she had never had anything for nothing. In Wybong she had lived and loved but she had also worked . . . and worked—and worked.

Oh dear, she thought, as she put the tray in the pantry, I'm not allowed to talk about Wybong and I'll have to stop thinking about it. Millicent was right when she said Wybong was not Two Creeks. It was at Two Creeks she would have to learn to live and work—and work—and work.

Oliver, having hung his hat, stood quite still in the passage. He took out a cigarette and lit it. As he did so he listened to Carey's footsteps fading away down the hall. His eyes were tired. Then with a fine frown between his brows he went towards his study. Millicent could not be thwarted and she would have to be endured.

As he went in Millicent was standing behind his table, leafing through the envelopes brought in with the mail. She picked up a pamphlet and sitting down in Oliver's chair began to look through it. She did not look up as she went on. "I'm here this week to put the place in order ready for the gymkhana influx. And, of course, the annual gathering of the Shire Council and their wives. By the way," she looked up, "you will be the next president as a matter of course, I suppose?"

Oliver walked over to the window and stood looking out. Carey had come around the side veranda and had jumped down on to the path below it. Tony had just come through the side garden gate.

"I suppose so," Oliver said, referring to Millicent's remark about being President of the Shire Council.

"You do realise, of course, that the president needs some well-trained support from his wife? It's probably quite an art handling all the councillors' wives. Then there is committee work . . ."

"That is something of which you have been reminding me for years, my dear Millicent. I now have a wife. You can cease to worry."

Millicent got up from her chair, came round the table and went to Oliver's side.

"My dear brother," she said in a tone that manifestly

showed she was trying to hide her exasperation, "Carey is very inexperienced. I think I should be here . . . at her side."

Oliver did not reply.

"You are not paying attention to me, Oliver," she went on. "What are you looking at so intently?"

She moved a curtain aside with one finger.

Tony had climbed into the pepper tree and Carey stood beneath it, her face upturned, watching the boy. She was smiling and one hand was lifted, pointing to something in the tree. The curve of her throat, the lifted arm, the tilt of her head, emphasised the slender youthful curves of her body.

Oliver stubbed out his cigarette in an ash-tray on the table by the window ledge without taking his eyes from the scene in the garden. Millicent heard the faint bite of his teeth, almost as if he had clenched them together. She loked quickly at her brother. He was frowning.

Millicent let the curtain drop back into its place.

"I don't believe you are paying any attention to me," she said again, turning away. She sat down in a chair across the room, crossed her ankles and helped herself to a cigarette.

"Oliver," she said peremtorily, "will you please come to life and listen to me. You've got enormous responsibilities as President of the Shire Council. . . ."

Oliver turned round.

"Supposing we worry about that when the time comes," he said, going to his desk and himself now leafing through the mail. "What sort of a trip did you have out of Melbourne, Millicent, and how is Mother?"

Millicent watched her brother for a few minutes in silence. He did not appear to notice she was not answering his questions. He slit open a letter with a paper-knife and read it. As he read he frowned.

"You must be tired, Oliver," Millicent said. "Why don't you sit down and read your mail?

"Oliver," she said loudly and firmly. "Two things are of importance. The curtains have to be taken down, dry cleaned and replaced in the next two weeks. And we have visitors for the week-end. Has that penetrated, because you are clearly not in a listening mood."

"Leave the curtains to Carey," said Oliver, not looking

up. "And I know about the visitors. Jane Newbold and a Mr. Harry Martin from Wybong."

"What a combination!" said Millicent with a disdainful laugh.

Oliver looked up over the letter he was holding in his hand. He was still standing.

"I'd be grateful if you'd keep your feelings on the subject of Jane and Harry Martin from Carey," he said.

Millicent knew what that hard cold light in Oliver's eyes usually meant.

"That, I suppose, is what you intend to do?" she said.

"If I had feelings about them that is what I would do," said Oliver quietly.

Millicent gave a little deprecating laugh.

"My dear Oliver," she said. "It is when you have feelings that you put up that ice-cold façade. I know you better than you think. As for the curtains, Carey wouldn't dream of interfering in something about which she knows nothing."

She went out and closed the door quietly. Oliver went on slitting envelopes and letting his eyes flick through the contents. He put the last of the letters in a pile at the side of the blotting pad and a paper-weight on them. He went back to the window.

Night had come down swiftly with the going of the sun and nothing could be seen in the garden now. He drew the curtain, went out of the study and upstairs to his room. Ten minutes later the water could be heard pouring from the shower-room.

CHAPTER TEN

Oliver, in spite of his lateness, was the first downstairs and as neither Carey nor his sister were there he went once again to his study. He picked up one of the letters that had come in with the mail and carried it into the small room adjoining. He put it on a ledge while he took down the pedigree book from a shelf.

The door was ajar, leaving a wide crack through which he could see part of his study, particularly the part that showed the corner of the big table on which the telephone rested. He heard a slight tap on his study door but he did not lift his head or answer it. He was busy.

It was Carey who came into the study and went to the chair at the side of the table near the telephone. She lifted the receiver and asked the exchange for long distance.

Oliver looked up. Carey, through the crack, was sitting with both elbows on the table, resting her chin in one hand and holding the telephone receiver with the other. She was obviously waiting for long distance to come through on the line. Oliver bent his head and went on checking his pedigree reference.

He lifted his head with some surprise when the number was connected and Carey asked for Mrs. Cleaver. He then could see she had a note-book in front of her.

"It's Carey, Mrs. Cleaver . . . I want you to do something for me if you will? . . . It might be a little trouble but you see I had to ask you because it's a matter of *taste* and I just couldn't leave it to a store, even a good store."

Oliver bent his head to his book again. Women's affairs!

He lifted his head sharply when he heard Carey giving measurements of rooms, of window frames, and details of furniture and colours in some of the upstairs rooms. He looked through the crack and could see the tiny frown of concentration on Carey's face as she consulted her note-book.

"If you go to the store straight away and tell them it is urgent they'll send them out express. They did for Oliver, before I was married . . . You will? Oh, you are a darling. You see I have to have them before the others come back from the dry cleaners and up before . . . well, before Millicent *minds*. You do know what I mean, don't you? You do understand? . . . You see, if I just start with one or two rooms and let Millicent do the others we'll both be happy."

Oliver could see Carey's face suffused with a glow. The light from the overhead bracket shone down on her and caught the glint of sudden unshed tears.

"Oh, Mrs. Cleaver, I would so love you to come and see me sometime . . . Could I ring you up when you're not so busy?"

She put the receiver back on its rest and sat looking at it. Then she lifted her hand and wiped a tear from the corner of one eye.

Oliver took a step and opened the door wide. Carey looked up to see him standing there, the letter in one hand.

"Oh, Oliver . . ." she said. "I didn't know you were there."

"I'm sorry to have been an unconscious listener," he said. "I thought you were probably ringing through on some business. I'm afraid I overheard you." He crossed the short space to his table and put the pedigree book and the letter down. "What goes on about the curtains?" he asked.

"Well, you see . . ." she said. "Well, Oliver, you did want me not to let Millicent be too busy, didn't you? I didn't want to upset her though. I thought if I just began with one or two rooms. . . . Of course I wouldn't dream of replacing the curtains in the big downstairs rooms, or in here. They are beautiful curtains, anyway. The ones upstairs are good, too . . . but I just had to show my metal . . . as it were . . . somewhere."

She looked anxiously at Oliver as if expecting his censure.

"Go on," he said quietly.

"Well, you see . . . when the curtains come down to go to the dry cleaners I'll put my new ones up in the two side upstairs rooms instead of the old ones when they come back. I'll have made a beginning, won't I? I mean about managing things myself. Sort of inch by inch, if you know what I mean?"

What clear eyes he had! How directly he always looked at people and things. She had never really looked right into his eyes. There was a fine dark ring round the grey. That was what made the white part of his eyes seem so very white.

Suddenly Carey knew she had been looking into Oliver's eyes too long. She blinked. Then looked down at her notebook.

"Mrs. Cleaver would like to come and stay on Two Creeks for a few days . . . later. She's booked up just now. And I would like her to come. I would so very much, Oliver. . . ."

She looked up again quickly, again seeking his approval. To her surprise his eyes had softened. Carey's heart leapt. For the first time they were nearly smiling at one another; their eyes were meeting and something of understanding was passing between them.

He only had to put out his hand and perhaps some of the barriers would be down.

"You go right ahead and do just what you want to do about the curtains, Carey. They are your curtains, you

know. Two Creeks homestead is your homestead. . . ."
He paused. "And I'd be delighted for your sake if Mrs.
Cleaver came to us for a visit."

"Oh, thank you so much."

"Don't thank me, Carey. I want you to be happy."
He bent his head while he took a cigarette from the box
and lit it. "Quite a busy time you'll be having with visitors
in the next few weeks," he said through the smoke drift
of his cigarette. "There's Harry Martin. . . ."

He watched the eagerness in Carey's face as she said,
"Oh, yes. You'll like Harry, Oliver. I love him. He's a
darling."

Oliver's eyes went back to the cigarette he was holding
in his hand.

"He was something special in that life back there in
Wybong?"

"More than that. When I was ever so young I used
to think I'd marry Harry when I grew up. I was always
longing to hurry and grow up. I was always telling Harry
I was hurrying as fast as I could . . . and to wait for me."
She laughed.

"And didn't he?" asked Oliver.

"He never asked me," said Carey. "Well," she added,
laughingly, "I suppose I didn't give him a chance, did I?
I married you."

"And left poor Harry standing?"

"Oh, no. He's my best friend. He wouldn't come down
here to help me with my farm if he didn't still like me.
Oliver, you don't think Harry is just a fencer, do you?
Millicent is afraid he's only a workman. He's not. He's a
contractor and in Wybong he's very important."

"Very important to you, too!" said Oliver dryly. He
shook the ash from his cigarette into the ash-tray. "Don't
worry, I won't let Millicent cast him out with the roustabouts.
We'll have to hope for the best with Millicent and Jane.
By the way, did you know that Millicent is bringing Jane
Newbold here at the end of the week?"

Carey could feel iron bands were tightening round her
heart.

Why hadn't he told her about Jane Newbold coming when
Jane must have arranged it with him that day she called
in at Two Creeks? And did they all really think that anyone
from Wybong was bound to be a country hick with whom they
would put up for Carey's sake?

"Harry is the finest man I've ever met," Carey said, her thoughts leaving Jane for the moment. "He's very good-looking, and well dressed. Even the people on the big stations defer to Harry Martin."

Oliver's eyebrows flickered. His eyes grew remote again.

"I have every confidence in your good taste, my dear child. You do not have to defend Mr. Martin to me. I'm concerned only with Millicent and Jane. I want peace there, too. . . ."

"Oh, you'll have that," Carey said, rising. "I'll see to that, Oliver. Jane will be charming to you . . . quite naturally. It is no effort for Jane to be charming. And Millicent will be busy with the curtains. . . ."

She could not keep the faintly bitter note from her voice. A few minutes ago she had glimpsed heaven. Now she saw only icy winter in Oliver's face. And he had called her *my dear child*.

On Monday morning the curtains were down and the temporary ones up in their place while the good ones were dispatched in the utility truck to the dry cleaners at Preston, the nearest Shire town.

On the morning after Millicent's arrival Carey said:

"You look tired, Millicent. You must be awfully glad to get out to the country to have a rest."

"Of course I'm tired," Millicent said. "But I haven't time to rest." And she had gone on bustling about the place, going through Hannah's inventory of silver; the book-keeper's stock book in the station store, and supervising the pulling down of the curtains.

At morning tea-time Carey said:

"Do sit down for your tea, Millicent. You need the rest, you know. You'll be able to do ever so much more if you are rested."

Then when they sat down she asked Millicent about her Melbourne activities during the preceding week.

"No wonder you look so tired," she said sympathetically. "You deserve some cosseting. A rest and a little spoiling is what you need. I don't suppose anyone has ever really given you the treats you are always wearing yourself out giving to others."

It took two days of loving kindness and sympathy to convince Millicent that that was just what she needed and deserved.

"Really," she said on the third morning when she sat down for morning tea, "I've *had* it. Looking after Cranston and Two Creeks is more than I ought to have to bear. I really should come here for a holiday and not for work. Carey, do you think you could see that Hannah puts all that silver back? And do see that there isn't one single smudge on *one* piece."

"Yes, of course I will, Millicent. If you put your feet up on that foot-rest you'll find it more comfortable to read a magazine. I expect those magazines that come regularly are your order."

Carey took the tea things quietly away in the direction of the pantry.

On Thursday and Friday Millicent had got the habit of being the *prima donna* who needed cosseting and it was amazing how Hannah, Cook and the roustabout all vied with one another to see she was well cosseted, on her favourite lounge on the front veranda.

Out of sheer loyalty Carey said nothing to Hannah or Cook, but one or twice their eyes met. Carey would not let her eyes speak for her but she knew there was infinite relief in their hearts that Millicent was no longer going through the nooks and crannies of Two Creeks like a spring wind.

The first indication of Harry Martin's arrival was a telephone call from Tim Wackett down at the stables

"We've just had a telephone call through from the railhead at Preston asking us to send out a horse-box for three ponies on the freight train from Albury, Mrs. Reddin. Seems like they're consigned to you. The stationmaster says there's a man travelling along with them."

Carey had been passing through the passage with a vase of flowers in her hand when the telephone rang. At the news that those three brumbies had come after all she would have wrung her hands except that she had the telephone receiver in one hand and the flowers in the other.

"Oh, Tim," she cried, "it's Harry Martin. Are you sure there are some horses, too?"

"All I know is they've asked us to send out a horse-box or get Smithson in Preston to bring 'em out."

"Could you . . . I mean, would you send a box, Tim?"

"Surely, if that's what you want. Can't ask Mr. Oliver.

102

He's gone into Preston himself in the big car. He's gone to meet the up train for some engine parts wanted on the refrigeration plant."

"Then please do that. And Tim? Could I go, too? I mean in the horse-box with your driver?"

"I guess so, only there won't be room for three on the road out. I suppose that Harry Martin is coming right along to Two Creeks. Maybe if you could pick up Mr. Oliver in Preston there'd be room for the extra passenger in his car."

"We could try. If we don't . . . well, I'm very small. I suppose I could squeeze in between Harry and the driver. That is, if your driver doesn't mind."

Tim Wackett on the other end of the phone laughed.

"The driver won't mind. How about this Harry Martin?"

"Oh, he won't mind," said Carey confidently. "He'd do anything for me."

"Right-oh then! Can you be down at the stables in half an hour?"

"Yes, I'll be there, Tim."

Tony had come into the passage at the sound of Carey's voice. He was sucking his pencil and listening with interest.

"Can I come too, Carey?"

"Don't say 'can.' Say 'may,' Tony. No, darling. There's hardly room for me and certainly not for a small boy."

"I can ride in the box with the horses."

"Not brumbies, darling. They've got wicked hooves and bad manners. Besides, you've got to get on with your work."

Tony kicked one foot against the other.

"Don't be tough, Carey. Please—please . . ."

"No wheedling. Listen, you finish your work and be down at the stables to meet us when we get back. You're going to like Harry Martin, and don't forget you're going to work with him. On *our* farm."

Tony considered.

"Oh . . . all right. I suppose," he said turning away. "Only don't let Millicent get in my way while I'm busy, will you?"

"Darling, she's had breakfast in bed to-day . . . ready for the visit of Miss Jane Newbold. Supposing you keep out of her way for a change?"

Tony looked balefully over his shoulder at Carey.

"I suppose when this Harry Martin comes you'll be too busy for me any more."

Carey put the vase of flowers down on the floor and knelt down by Tony. She put her arms around him.

"Never, Tony," she said. "*Never*."

She couldn't tell him he was necessary to her because he was someone to love in the kind of way that meant she could put her arms around someone and press a small head to her heart and drop heartfelt kisses on a waiting forehead.

Funny, but Tony was the only person she had ever really kissed.

When Carey had left Wybong she had kissed sundry people on the brow . . . and at her wedding. She hadn't even kissed Oliver at her wedding.

What would *really* kissing someone, with the love pouring out from one's heart, be like?"

Carey had forgotten Tony. Guiltily she sprang to her feet.

"Run along, Tony darling," she said. "Be seeing you . . . down at the stables. What time will we get back from Preston, Tony? How far is it?"

Tony liked being appealed to as an authority.

"Four o'clock this afternoon . . . if you drive in quickly. It isn't how far it is. It's that you can't drive horse-boxes with horses in 'em fast on that track."

"Thank you, darling. I don't know what I'd do if I didn't have you to teach me."

She picked up the flowers and hurrying into the dining-room put them on the sideboard.

She ran lightly upstairs and put on another more becoming blue dress and a small hat with a fluted brim. She looked quickly at herself in the mirror.

"I'll do," she thought. "But I do want Harry to think I look well, and happy."

She dusted her nose with powder and ran out of the room and down the staircase.

It was close on midday when they got into Preston. The driver drove the horse-box straight into the railway yards where it took only a moment's glance to see where the flats and stock trucks consigned to Preston had been shunted on to a side line.

Carey hurried along the dirt track beside the railway line, looking for the box-car that might be carrying the horses. Harry was too fond of his horses to be far away from them.

Though she glanced towards the consignment sheds in case Harry might be waiting in the shade there she failed to see the figure of her husband sitting on a packing-case a few yards inside the shadowed shed.

Oliver, his knees crossed, his hat on the case beside him, was talking to a railway official.

The figure of a young woman walking quickly down beside the railway line was unusual enough to attract anybody's attention. Oliver turned his head and then he stopped in the middle of what he was saying.

He dropped his cigarette on to the rough cement floor and ground it out with his heel.

" Sorry," he said to the man with him. " What was it you were saying?"

" Road transport could have brought this stuff in shorter time for you, Mr. Reddin, like you say. It was just bad luck it was consigned too late to catch the up train on Wednesday. If you could get your agent . . ."

He too stopped. Then went on:

" What the devil's that girl doing wandering round those horse trucks? Don't she know members of the public aren't allowed inside the railway yards?"

" Perhaps she is meeting someone," Oliver said evenly.

" There's only horses in those trucks. Oh, yeah . . . crikey! She's meeting someone all right."

The railway man allowed himself a crackle of humorous laughter.

" Bang into his arms. Kissing in broad daylight! Well, well, well!"

He laughed again.

" We'd better go and see if they're through checking those cases for me," Oliver said.

" You want a porter, Mr. Reddin?"

" I'll send a man up from the agency to collect the cases and put them in the back of my car. Is there a way out into the street through the shed?"

" Yeah. Just keep going ahead past the big boxes, then turn left off the goods office. They'll fix your freight check for you over there."

" Thanks very much," Oliver said. He walked abruptly away.

The railway man shook his head.

"Nice chap, Mr. Reddin," he said to his off-sider. "But love's just no topic that interests him. Couldn't see anything funny in that pair standing there in the middle of a railway line kissing one another. What do you know? It takes all sorts to make a world. And he's just married, so they say."

Oliver walked out of the street entrance of the goods office and across the road to where he had parked his car. He got in, started up the engine. He looked back to check the rear traffic before he pulled out into the street, moved into top and drove quickly into the centre of the town.

CHAPTER ELEVEN

Preston was like any other western town where the pursuits of its inhabitants were exclusively attached to the pastoral industry. There was a wide dusty main street and under the pepper trees towards its centre were wooden seats where the white-haired sages and old-timers held daily consultation on the state of the nation.

One side of the street was lined with veranda-shaded pastoral agencies, and in a row were the four main banks operating in the state. At the corner was the court-house and the police station, separated by a new modern garage rich with a growth of bowsers forming a barricade between the footpath and the garage proper. On the other side of the road was the main store of Preston which dealt in everything from gum-boots to sewing-machines.

On the corner, next to the store, was the hotel. It had had a modern frontage attached to it in recent years and it now sported a glass-walled lounge from the deep arm-chairs of which the occupants could watch the passers-by in the street. Next to the hotel, the last building in the town, was the stone and brick edifice of the Shire offices and the town library.

Oliver drove his car behind the line of bowsers in the garage, got out and shut the door with a bang. He spoke to the mechanic who came out to attend to him, then crossed the wide brown street to the Shire offices.

He had barely disappeared inside the main door of the Shire office when Jane Newbold drove in from the north end of the town and parked her car immediately behind Oliver's in the garage.

As the mechanic came towards her she nodded towards Oliver's car.

"Mr. Reddin's in town, I see," she said.

"Yes, miss. Been in an hour or more. Saw him come in round ten o'clock. He's just left the car for filling."

"Fill my car up, will you?" Jane asked, getting out. "Run it out on to the kerb when you're finished. I may be an hour or so." She looked up casually. "Did Mr. Reddin come in alone? I'm on my way out to Two Creeks now, so I'll look out for him."

"Yeah . . . he was alone. But I saw the Two Creeks horse-box come in about an hour later. Young lady in it. My boss said it was the new Mrs. Reddin."

"She wasn't *driving* it?"

"No, Jem Anderson was driving."

"Well, thanks very much."

She walked out on to the kerb and glanced up and down the street. She then turned south and walked the length of the main street, past the pepper trees and the old-timers; past the pastoral agency that handled the Two Creeks business. She glanced in but there was no sign of Oliver . . . or for that matter, Carey.

She crossed over the road and walked back to the hotel. She went into the lounge, chose herself a comfortable seat facing the window wall and ordered coffee.

As she lit a cigarette she looked up through the smoke haze and saw Carey walking along the opposite side of the main street beside a big broad-shouldered man in khaki clothes and wearing a wide-brimmed hat.

Jane could see that Carey, although she was on the far side of the man, was looking eagerly up into his face and that her hand clung to his arm and that she was talking quickly and excitedly.

Jane held the cigarette away from her and gazed over its spiral of smoke to the scene in the street. She could see the bench sitters leaning forward watching Carey and her companion going farther along the street. They continued to watch them, as Jane did, until they turned into Smithson's Stock Agency a little farther along.

"Well, that's not Jem Anderson," said Jane Newbold to herself. "Nor anyone else that I've ever seen on Two Creeks."

107

Across the road, at an angle, she saw the garage mechanic run Oliver's car, and then her own, out on to the street and park them one behind the other alongside the kerb under the pepper trees. Jane smiled.

"Oliver can't miss my car any more than I can miss his," she thought to herself.

She was sipping her coffee when Oliver came along the footpath under the hotel window from the direction of the Shire offices. His head was turned away as he looked across the street at the two cars drawn up bumper to bumper. Jane got up, took the few steps to the window and rapped hard on it. Oliver turned his head, saw Jane and raised his hat.

Jane smiled brilliantly at him and motioned with her hand for him to come and join her. For a fraction of a second he hesitated, then turned on his heel and retraced his steps to the hotel entrance. A minute later he was putting his hat on the table in the foyer and then came across the lounge to Jane.

"Hallo, old thing," she said. "How long will you be in town?"

Oliver reached the table and with a casual gesture Jane indicated the chair opposite her . . . one which had its back to the window.

"I'm ready to go back to Two Creeks as soon as they've delivered my engine parts to the car," he said. "And you? I suppose you've come through from Mount Macedon, Jane?"

"Yes, and I'm on my way to Two Creeks. They are expecting me, I hope?"

Oliver nodded.

"Millicent will have killed the fatted calf." He lifted his finger and signalled the steward. "I'll have tea, with some sandwiches. Jane?" He raised a quizzical eyebrow. "That looks like coffee you're drinking. May I order some more for you?"

"Please. With sandwiches this time. We might as well make it a light lunch and be done with it. I've been sitting here since your car was filled, Oliver. There's been no delivery to it. So you'll have time to have your tea leisurely." Oliver took out his cigarette-case and offered it to Jane. She shook her head.

"In five minutes' time," she said. "I'm not a chain smoker yet. . . ."

She laughed, and Oliver smiled.

"Is Carey with you?" Jane asked. "'By the way, who is the film star who walks along the street holding her hand? Big fellow who looks as if he's come from the desert centre?"

"That," said Oliver, lighting his cigarette and putting the spent match in the ash-tray, "is Mr. Harry Martin from Wybong. An old family friend."

"Not so old, *darling*. You could give him a few years. All the same, in an outback kind of way, he's rather attractive. Ah well . . . Carey's rather a sweet child." She stopped, looked straight into Oliver's eyes and said, "I suppose you've been married long enough to find that out. The very young can be very charming?"

Oliver's expression did not change.

"Did you enjoy your few days at Mount Macedon, Jane?"

"Yes. I had a lovely rest. Why did you change the subject, Oliver?"

"I think you know why."

"Yes . . . I think I do," said Jane. Then she laughed. "Come on, old thing, let me pour your tea for you. We're getting far too serious."

Over Oliver's shoulder she saw Carey and Harry Martin emerge from Smithson's Stock Agency and walk towards Oliver's car. Carey stood beside it a minute and looked up and down the street. Then she spoke to Harry Martin, obviously telling him to whom the car belonged.

Jane paid attention to the handing of Oliver's cup and saucer to him, and then pushed the sandwiches an inch nearer him.

"Tell me about the Shire Council, Oliver. You are to be the next president, aren't you?"

"It looks like it," Oliver said briefly.

"Carey wouldn't have had very much experience of town politics," Jane said with careful gentleness. "Even the old boys under the pepper trees can make or break a reputation in a country town. You'll have to tell Carey not to hold hands with an old family friend when she's the president's wife. At least not in the main street."

She could see Carey and Harry get into Smithson's utility which the agent had just driven into the street. The utility drove off in the direction of the railway yards.

"*Oliver* . . ." she said in a tone that commanded his eyes to meet hers. "I'm sorry I behaved the way I did at your wedding. I was jealous. You knew that, didn't you? Well, the past is the past. We won't speak of it again. You will let me help Carey if it's necessary, won't you? I have got the social know-how, you know."

"Carey has a way of managing her own affairs," Oliver said. "She seems to fill in her time quite happily at Two Creeks. And now she is likely to be absorbed in the refencing of her own farm. You know that Carey is a property owner in her own right, Jane?"

"Yes, I do," Jane said. The steward had brought her fresh coffee and she now poured it. "Hence Mr. Martin?"

"Hence Mr. Martin."

"Oh, well . . ." said Jane, with a laugh. "That's the way of life, isn't it? Do you suppose they want us to wait for them before we return to Two Creeks?"

"Unless they see me or my car in town they probably don't know I'm here. Carey came in to meet Mr. Martin after I left Two Creeks. They're probably lunching with a crate of wild horses down at the railway yards."

"By the way, Oliver," Jane said, glancing through the window, "there's a truck pulled up in front of your car and a man has opened the boot of it."

Oliver turned round in his seat and looked through the window behind him.

"That's what I've been waiting for. I can leave any time now. How about you, Jane?" He turned back to her. "Would you rather do some shopping and follow later?"

"Darling, if I can't have your company . . . I'll take your dust," Jane said, laughing. "Have you finished your lunch, Oliver? You haven't had much."

"All I want, thank you. If you're ready we can leave in the next ten minutes. If you'll excuse me, Jane, I'll just go across the street and see that stuff stowed properly. If you pull out your car I'll follow you." He was standing now and his smile as he looked down at Jane was faintly ironic. "I'm afraid chivalry demands that I take your dust, Jane, and not you mine."

"On your way, Sir Galahad," she laughed. "Give me fifteen minutes and two miles. I'll see you at Two Creeks for dinner."

Jane watched him cross the road and speak to the truck driver who had just finished loading into the boot of his car. Then he went on down the street to his own agency.

Jane went upstairs to the bathroom, rinsed her hands and remade up her face. When she was satisfied with what she saw in the mirror she retraced her steps back to the lounge and looked through the window. Oliver had not yet returned to his car.

She left the hotel, got into her own car and drove off, turned down a side street, swung right again along the railway line in the direction of the railway yards. Smithson's grazing paddocks were on the far side of the shunting lines.

She could see three figures . . . Carey, Harry Martin and the agent Smithson leaning over the gate of the grazing paddock gazing at three horses grouped a few yards away.

Jane slowed down to a crawl so that she would pass the gate at a slow pace. When she drew level she braked suddenly as if this was an unexpected stop. She leaned across the passenger seat behind her and called out.

"Hallo there, Car-eey. What goes on?"

Carey turned round. She hesitated for a moment and then crossed the grass verge to Jane's car.

"Just trying to make a bargain with Mr. Smithson," she said.

"Hard going?"

"Oh, no. He wants my horses but he's pretending not to want them. I don't want to part with them either. Silly, I suppose. Are you going out to Two Creeks now, Jane?"

"Right away. Want a lift?"

Carey looked uncertainly at the two men still standing by the gate.

"I think I'll wait and go with Harry," she said. "It's a bit of a tight squeeze but Harry won't mind. I saw Oliver's car in the main street and wondered. . . ."

"Oh, he'll be gone by now," Jane said airily. "We had lunch together. Very nice to have Oliver to myself for a few minutes. He's so busy, isn't he? He was on his way back to Two Creeks as I left the hotel."

"I see," said Carey thoughtfully. Then she looked up and smiled gravely. "Thank you for the offer of a lift, Jane. I think I'll go with Harry. He hasn't been to Two Creeks before."

With a smooth glide the car moved forward. Carey stood watching it with a slightly worried frown on her forehead. Harry Martin left the fence and came over to her.

"What's the matter, Carey girl?" he said. "You don't

look as if that lady left you too happy. Who is she . . . besides being a glamour queen?"

"A friend of Millicent's," said Carey, then added slowly: "And Oliver's too, of course."

She looked up into Harry Martin's quizzical eyes and smiled.

"I was worrying because we hadn't really waited for Oliver, or gone looking for him when we saw his car in the main street. Perhaps we should have done that, Harry, but I . . . well . . . I did want to find someone to graze those ponies for me first. Then I could tell Oliver everything was all right about them."

Harry Martin was a tall broad-shouldered man in his late twenties. His eyes were the faded blue of the outback man and they had a certain lazy easy-going expression in them. He smiled broadly now, showing a very good set of white teeth.

"That husband of yours certainly must have something, Carey. You're so anxious to please him. How do I get a wife I can wrap round my little finger? That fellow seems to have all the luck."

He turned round and let his gaze move slowly over the paddocks where the brumbies were now quietly grazing.

"They seem to be okay there, Carey," he said, nodding his head in the direction of the horses. "Smithson's grazing charges are a bit steep . . . by Wybong standards . . . but it'll give us a breathing space to look over those paddocks of yours. Well, now we're through how about going home, eh?"

"We'll have to go back and get Jem and the horse-box. Thank you for paying for Jem's lunch, Harry. I never thought to bring any money with me. . . ."

"Like most station people, hey? Never have any time for money. Just stick it on the account, or get the agent to foot the bill?" He laughed teasingly.

"Well, one doesn't use money on a station, does one? I mean there's nothing to spend it on. At Two Creeks everything is got out of the station store or sent out from Melbourne."

"Who is Reddin's pastoral agent, Carey? There must be a representative in this town. There always is, in every country town. And you ought to carry your cheque-book. You have got one, haven't you, Carey?"

"Do you know I've never asked Oliver who his agent

is," Carey said. "It just wasn't necessary, Harry. Oliver looks after everything."

As they walked back to Smithson's utility Harry Martin noticed that Carey had not answered his question about the cheque-book.

Paying for Jem Anderson's lunch was nothing . . . but he couldn't quite get over the look of anxiety in Carey's eyes when she had realised that once in a country town she needed money. Not much, but enough for this and that. And she had become more than anxious when it was clear that Smithson wanted time to think over whether he would buy the brumbies or not. He would charge for the grazing in the meantime.

Harry chewed his bottom lip as they drove back into the railway yards to pick up the horse-box. He wondered what sort of a set-up it was out there at Two Creeks. He understood quick enough that a man who had a state-wide name for his stud stock would be chary of bringing brumbies on the place, but he didn't understand the half-hidden anxiety in Carey. Carey was a girl who always looked happy and sunny back home. Was it the different climate down here that had caught her off her beat?

If anyone out there at Two Creeks was making Carey unhappy then, by golly, they'd have Harry Martin to reckon with. Harry Martin was a busy man with big contract deals on hand. No one on earth but Carey Fraser would have got him out of the Wybong district right now.

Sitting there in the front seat of the horse-box as it rocketed over the uneven track to Two Creeks, Harry put his arm round Carey's shoulder and gave her a hug.

"Nice seeing you again, Carey," he said, smiling down at her where she sat happily squeezed between himself and the driver.

Carey smiled back at him.

"You too, Harry," she said.

She slipped her hand into his when he let his own fall from her shoulder. Harry held it firmly and Carey let it lie confidently there all the rest of the way to Two Creeks.

CHAPTER TWELVE

When Carey and Harry Martin walked up from the stables to the homestead they could see Oliver's big car at rest in the open garage. Jane's car was beside it. The other big homestead car had been moved over to another corner of the shed and Millicent's car lay behind it.

"Quite a fleet," said Harry, looking at them. "Lot of money in those big cars. You must have married a rich man, young Carey?"

"Well, I wouldn't really know. It's not the sort of thing we discuss. It's all taken for granted, Harry. But I do think that Two Creeks as a property is awfully wealthy. Doesn't it look like it to you?"

"I've been whistling under my breath ever since we turned off the track into the main gates," he said. "That blue car is the one the very glamorous lady with the red hair was driving, isn't it?"

"Yes, the one beside Oliver's car. She's staying with us, Harry, for a few days. I do hope you'll get on. And with Millicent, too." She looked up at him pleadingly.

"You mean I'm not to give them any outback back-chat if they put on too many airs . . . hey?" He was laughing down at her but behind the lazy good humour in his eyes there was an inquiring gleam.

"Please, Harry. Everyone here is different. But nicely different when you get to know them. One just has to get to know them. . . ."

"And how am I to greet that husband of yours? Tell him he pinched my girl? Offer to knock him down if he's a wife beater?" He was really laughing now.

"He's not the sort of person anyone talks to that way," Carey explained. "You'll see for yourself. And you'll like him. I know you'll like him. He's an awfully good pastoralist, and, Harry, you always admired a man who was a good pastoralist, didn't you?"

Harry put his arm around Carey's shoulder again.

"So that's it, is it? I've got to admire him *professionally*. Okay . . . okay. I'm admiring him already, on your recommendation."

They went through the garden and up the veranda steps.

Oliver, Millicent and Jane were sitting in an arm-chair group behind the trellis of creepers. As Carey and Harry came up the steps Oliver rose from his chair. He put his glass down on the table, his cigarette in the ash-tray, and came forward to meet them. His smile was polite and formal but when he shook Harry Martin's hand his grip was firm.

"I'm very glad you've arrived safely," he said. "I'm sorry I didn't know you'd be here to-day until I was in Preston myself this morning. Have you had a good trip?"

"I'm very glad to meet you, Mr. Reddin," said Harry. His grip was equally firm.

"Will you come and sit down," Oliver said. "We're just having a sundowner. You must meet my sister. Millicent, this is Mr. Harry Martin. Miss Newbold."

Carey was so anxious that these two men should like one another, that the first moments should be the best moments, that she did not notice that Oliver had neither looked at her nor addressed her. She stood a little back from the group, her eager face turned first to one then the other as Oliver performed the introductions. She saw that Millicent and Jane were looking at Harry curiously and that Millicent, the always perfect Reddin, stood up, shook hands with a kind of remote graciousness and said:

"Please sit here, Mr. Martin."

It was an order as well as a request and Harry moved towards the chair on the far side of the one Oliver had been sitting in. But he did not sit down. He was waiting for Carey to sit down, too.

Oliver moved behind another chair on the other side of the table from his own. He stood behind it and put one hand on its back rest.

"Will you sit down, Carey? I will get Hannah to bring some drinks out."

The glance he gave her was fleeting and impersonal but he held the chair for her while she sat down. Carey was too used to that impersonal manner to notice that it was more marked to-day.

She sat down in order that Harry might do so but she would rather have gone upstairs and had a bath and dressed. Jane and Millicent were both so very bathed, brushed, dressed and at ease.

Her glance went gratefully to Harry who had sat down, accepted a cigarette from Oliver and was perfectly at ease. Jane did not miss the glance they exchanged. She tried to exchange one with Millicent but at that moment Millicent was turning to speak to Hannah who had come out on the veranda.

"Will you bring the tray with all the drinks on out here, Hannah? It's so warm this evening I think we'll stay here until dinner."

"Yes, Miss Millicent," Hannah said submissively and then as she seemed to hesitate Millicent asked:

"What is it, Hannah? Is there something you want?"

"Only a message for Miss Carey . . ." She looked anxiously towards Carey. "It's Tony. He's had an accident. Oh, nothing much, but I put him to bed on the back veranda next to Cook's room. He made such a fuss he wouldn't go down to Wackett's cottage."

Carey had risen from her chair.

"He cut his leg, Miss Carey. Right down the shin bone. There was blood everywhere but Mr. Oliver said it didn't need stitching."

Jane Newbold laughed.

"Oliver and his *dependants*," she said. "Really, how he does clutter himself up."

Carey had turned to go inside and as Jane spoke their eyes met. Carey knew without any shadow of doubt that that was exactly how Jane classed her, Carey.

"Excuse me please, everyone," said Carey. "I won't be long."

As she hurried into the house she heard Oliver's firm resonant voice asking Harry what he liked to drink . . . and Millicent saying to Jane, "That child is always under somebody's feet. He ought to be sent to a home."

Carey went quickly through the hall, down the side passage and through the breakfast-room to the back veranda. Tony was sitting up in bed reading a comic.

"Tony!" said Carey, both relieved and exasperated. Tony was so very much alive and enjoying himself . . . and for a moment she had panicked. "Tony, where did you get all those comics?"

"Mrs. Wackett. Mrs. Byron from Hilldale was visiting her and she brought them for me. They were Don Byron's and he's finished with them."

"Does Mr. Oliver know you've got them?"

"Yes. He told me to bury myself in them so as he won't hear or see me again for the next twenty-four hours. He's pretty mad, Carey."

116

Carey sat down on the end of the bed, picked up one of the comics and saw at a glance it was a good type and put it down.

"Tony, darling, why is he mad, and what did you do?"

"Well, he came in from Preston just after Miss Newbold, and he was just sitting down to have a get-together with her on the veranda when I fell off the balustrade on the side veranda. He was black as thunder. . . ."

"I expect he was upset because you had fallen and hurt yourself."

"No he wasn't. It was because I had dropped the binoculars too. He was really mad, Carey. He said they weren't ever to be touched by anyone. He didn't care how much I was bleeding because he had to see the binoculars were all right first."

"Darling, what were you doing standing on the balustrade with the binoculars?"

"Watching for you to come. Did you bring me anything from Preston? Mrs. Wackett always brings me fruit balls from the store."

"No, Tony, I didn't. I'm so sorry. . . ."

Carey leaned forward and brushed a lock of hair back from Tony's forehead.

"Didn't you think about me?" Tony asked accusingly.

"I didn't have any money with me. I didn't even have any for Jem Anderson's lunch."

"Who paid for your lunch then?"

"Harry Martin. And Jem's, too. Tony, you wait till you see him. You'll love him, and he said it's all right for you to work on the fences when the gang comes in. He's going to tell them you're to have a job. . . .?"

"Why don't you ever have any money, Carey? You didn't have any the day we went into Ballarat. Don't you ever have any?"

"No," said Carey very quietly. She stood up and bent over Tony and kissed his forehead. Her voice brightened. "Nobody wants money on a station. Everything's provided. If Oliver bandaged your leg I expect it's done very efficiently."

"Too right. And he hurt. But I think he was kinda sorry afterwards though he wouldn't say so. He didn't say 'No' when Cook said she'd bath me and put me to bed here. And when Mrs. Wackett brought up the comics he said I could have them."

"Of course he would be sorry. He's really a kind man

117

underneath." She moved away towards the door into the breakfast-room. " I have to bath and get dressed, Tony. . . ."

" Oh, yes, and look your best for Harry Martin," Tony said jealously.

" And for you too, dear."

" Miss Newbold said Mr. Oliver's kind," Tony said across the width of the veranda. " He puts up with me and you, and we're both orphans. So I guess he is . . ."

" Yes, he loves us both," Carey said weakly, then under her breath offered a prayer to God that he would forgive her the lie.

Carey went down the hall towards the front entrance to explain to the others that she was going to dress for dinner, and suggest that Hannah be allowed to show Harry to his room. As she neared the open front door she heard a burst of Harry Martin's laughter. Then Millicent's voice, followed by Jane's which sounded gay and animated. Then she heard Oliver asking Harry if he would have another drink.

Carey hesitated before she reached the front door. They sounded so happy, so self-contained. They were enjoying themselves. Yes, truly, the arrival of visitors to Two Creeks had brought vitality in its train. She was relieved that Harry was evidently a success.

She turned to meet Hannah who was carrying a plate of canapés towards the veranda.

" Will you ask Mr. Oliver if you can show Mr. Martin his room when they're ready, Hannah?" she said. " I'm going up to change now."

" Yes, I will do that, Miss Carey. You do look tired. See if you can get a half-hour nap before you come down. I'll hold the fort downstairs."

" Of course you will, Hannah," Carey said gratefully. " I might just rest a little while."

She went upstairs and along the long passage that ran from front to back of the big homestead. At the head of the staircase she could see into the open door of Jane's room. Jane's cases were there and Jane's very frilly frothy blue nightgown was laid across the bed for all the world to see.

She had mental visions of Oliver and Jane passing one another to and from the bathroom in their dressing-gowns, Jane's dressing-gown a colour that would contrast with her hair, of course, and with cut and trimmings to accentuate her figure.

She opened her own bedroom door, and then stood still and gazed into it.

Oliver's discarded shirt lay across that other bed. His khaki trousers hung over the back of a chair. The dust-covered elastic-sided shoes he had worn into Preston were in the middle of the floor. On the dressing-table lay his tie . . . and his hair-brushes rested on their backs in front of the mirror.

She went into the room, closed the door and leaned back against it.

"What . . . whatever does that mean?" she thought.

She sat on the side of the bed and looked at Oliver's clothes. Presently she got up, picked up the things one by one and put them in a neat pile on the chair. Oliver's shoes she put side by side under the chair. She slipped off her own clothes and put on a gown, picked up her soap-box and towel and went down to the bathroom.

She stayed a long time in the bath. It was warm and comforting, and she was tired. Somehow she was afraid to go back to that room. It frightened her because there was all the evening to go through and she couldn't endure four hours of trying either to meet, or not to meet, Oliver's eyes.

Somehow it worried her more than if she had seen Oliver's clothes hanging up in Jane Newbold's room. If that had been the case she would have *known*. As it was . . . with them tossed around in her room . . . she didn't *know*. She didn't know anything. It meant everything, and it meant nothing.

At length Carey stepped out of the bath, dried herself slowly and took off the little cap she had put on to keep her hair dry. She ran the comb through her hair in front of the corner mirror, then cleaned her teeth. She put on her dressing-gown, picked up her slippers in her hand and padded barefooted down the long passage.

Harry's room at the far end had the light on and the door open now. She could hear him releasing the latches on his suitcase. There was a light under Millicent's door but not under Jane's door. There was a light under her own door. Had she left it on?

She turned the handle slowly and pushed the door open. Oliver was sitting on the bed by the window, smoking a cigarette. Her crystal pin tray was on the pillow and he was tipping his ash into it.

Carey stood uncertainly in the doorway. In her left hand she held her slippers and over her right arm was her towel.

"I—I forgot my soap-box," she said, turning. "I—I left it in the bathroom. . . ."

"Come in, Carey, and shut the door behind you. Damn your soap-box and stop looking as if you're about to faint."

Carey came in and shut the door. She walked with a slightly uneven tread towards the cupboard against the far wall. She hung her towel over the rail inside its door.

"I always look like that after I have a bath," she said. "People do when they wash their faces. Haven't you noticed? They look kind of white . . . It's the water, and the rubbing."

Oliver did not move. He sat, his knees crossed, the cigarette in one hand, and looked out of those hard clear eyes at Carey.

"Sit down on that bed over there," he said very quietly. "Tell me about going into Preston in the horse-box. And those brumbies. When did you know Harry Martin was ariving this morning?"

"I didn't know Harry was coming this morning until nine o'clock. I just didn't want the brumbies to come to Two Creeks. Harry missed my telegram at Albury. I wanted to get rid of them before you got mad about them. I wanted to sell them, too. I wanted some money."

"What on earth did you want money for?"

Carey looked gravely at Oliver.

"What does anyone want money for, Oliver? Don't you ever have any? Didn't you have to pay for Jane's lunch to-day?"

"Good heavens. A pound, or thirty shillings . . ." He stopped dead. "Carey," he said, "how much money have you got?"

"Well . . . not very much. I never do have much . . . I mean money doesn't matter very much . . ." she said, unaware she was contradicting herself.

"How much money have you got in your handbag this minute?"

"Well . . . none just now," she said.

"How much have you had in it since we were married?"

120

There was another tiny silence.

"Have you had any money in it at all, Carey?"

She shook her head.

There was an ominous note in Oliver's voice when he spoke.

"The day before we were married I opened a joint account in both our names in the Commonwealth Trading Bank. A cheque-book was issued for you and Millicent was to give it to you. Did you know that, Carey?"

She shook her head.

He stubbed out his cigarette in Carey's crystal pin tray and stood up with a sudden angry movement. He walked up and down the floor as if he was trying to control his anger before he trusted himself with words.

"I suppose you'll grow up some day, Carey," he said. "Why didn't you tell me you didn't have any money?"

"There are a lot of things I don't tell you, Oliver," Carey said quietly. "You don't seem to want to know anything very much about me."

"I don't . . ." He broke off abruptly. He took two steps and sat down on the bed opposite Carey again. He leaned forward. "What makes you think that?" he said slowly.

"You go away early in the morning. We haven't time to talk together."

"I'm here now. Let's talk together now."

"It's nearly dinner-time, Oliver. We have guests. . . ."

"Oh, yes . . . we have guests," Oliver said.

Carey's eyes went to Oliver's clothes neatly folded on the chair against the wall.

"You—you left your clothes in here, Oliver . . ." she said.

He stood up. He put one hand on one silk clad shoulder and then suddenly put the other hand on the other shoulder. He stood looking down at Carey's upturned face. It was shining from her bath and one lock of her hair had fallen across her forehead. His hands slipped down to her waist. Carey, looking up at him, wondered why his eyes were dark, for in another minute she thought he might really take her in his arms.

"You didn't think with a house full of people I was going to have any one of them think I didn't have a right to come into my wife's room, did you? That I am not master in my own home?" he said between half-closed lips.

Carey expelled her breath. To her it was like a long soundless wail.

"Oh, is that all?" she said. *It had only been for the look of it.* She drew back so that her body was no longer touching his. "Please take them away, Oliver. I don't—I don't want them there."

His eyes did not leave her eyes.

"You are still afraid of me, Carey, aren't you?

"You are very strange to me, Oliver. I do not understand you."

He dropped his hands and walked abruptly away from her. On the other side of the room he ran his fingers through his hair, and leaned his shoulder against the wall and looked at her. He looked as if he was going to say something, then instead he jerked himself upright again.

"As you say, Carey . . . we have guests. I trust you will look after Mr. Martin's well-being. I've no doubt Millicent will attend to Jane." He walked to the door and opened it. "I will see you later downstairs." He nodded his head towards the chair and its contents.

"Tell Hannah to get rid of that junk," he said, and went out.

CHAPTER THIRTEEN

The next morning only Carey, Oliver and Harry Martin presented themselves for breakfast. Jane and Millicent were both having a tray sent up to their rooms. Millicent had now accepted this as a right and not a privilege and she had persuaded Jane it was a more restful and far more *chic* thing to be waited on on a country property than get up with those who had the problems of hard work on their hands.

Carey was amazed at how easy this victory had been over Millicent. The latter would never dream it was a means of keeping her out of the way. She interpreted it as a gesture of her position in the house.

Oliver and Harry were still carefully and politely addressing one another as "Mr. Reddin" and "Mr. Martin." Carey could see that Oliver's manner, of one business man to another, was impeccable; and she could also see that in some oblique way Harry was impressed by Oliver. This gave her a great sense of relief and she felt grateful to them both.

If things kept on going this way perhaps the affairs of her farm would not be so very long in being put in order. How disastrous it would have been if Oliver and Harry had *not* been prepared to co-operate!

"I suggest you get Carey to take you over the property at once, Mr. Martin," Oliver said over the steak and eggs. "I'm sure your time is valuable."

Harry smiled across the table at Carey.

"That's why we're up with the birds, Mr. Reddin. However, as you're the executor of the estate I might need your advice. And, of course, I can't make any decisions or offer a tender without your okay. Are you pressed for time yourself this morning? The sooner the three of us get together on the place the better."

"Very well," Oliver said. "I'll have the utility brought up in half an hour. As soon as we've finished breakfast you might come to my study and I'll show you the plans of the estate and the ordnance office survey. The fences on the boundary road have been down so long they might need surveying with the Shire Council authority. We can get in a professional surveyor."

"I am a surveyor, Mr. Reddin."

Oliver looked up sharply.

"You are a surveyor?"

"That's my profession."

"I see."

"Harry can do anything," Carey said by way of explanation. "He surveys roads and lays them, too. He locates the boundaries of the big stations for the State Government and he . . ."

She broke off and her voice died away. Harry was looking at her with the old kindly grin but Oliver was paying attention to his toast. She was not sure he was listening to her at all. Suddenly she realised she had been speaking with a note of possessive pride, and perhaps it was embarrassing to Harry.

"Do you want me to come to the study to go over those plans too, Oliver?" she asked.

"Not necessarily, Carey." He looked up at her. "You might put in that odd half-hour rebinding Tony's leg."

Carey had already rebound Tony's leg but she did not say so. She interpreted Oliver's suggestion as an indirect way of telling her he wanted to confer with Harry alone.

"Yes, I'll see to Tony," she said willingly. She was terribly anxious that Harry should not think Oliver was dismissing her "When I hear the utility come up I'll go out to it."

After breakfast she sat on the edge of Tony's bed and told him what school work she thought he was quite well enough to do.

"But I'm sick to-day, Carey," Tony said, pulling a long face and trying to look sick.

"Only in your leg and not in your head, darling. Besides, you have to hurry up if you want to be my manager. You've an awful lot to learn quickly. You'll learn quickest and most from Harry Martin while he's here so you had better hurry up mending that leg, too."

"Does he know more than Mr. Oliver?"

Carey pursed up her lips, put her head on one side, and thought.

"About some things," she said at length. "Then Oliver knows more about other things."

"If they both put their heads together they'd know an awful lot about most things?"

Carey smiled.

"That's what I thought, Tony. That's why I wanted Harry Martin to come and help me with my farm. But I was keeping it a secret."

"From Mr. Oliver?"

"Yes, but you've guessed it. You won't tell, will you, Tony?"

"You're an awful cunning one, Carey."

"I know. But then I had to be cunning to manage all those men back there in Wybong. My Uncle Tam took the most managing . . . but there were lots more. . . ."

"Why don't you manage Mr. Oliver then?"

"I don't really know, Tony," she said sadly. "Somehow with Oliver I seem to have lost my gift."

"He manages you, that's why," Tony said sagaciously.

Out of the mouths of babes . . . Carey thought, but she smiled brightly at the boy.

"I guess that's the way women are made. I can hear the utility now. I'll have to go, darling . . . be good and do your work. Maybe to-morrow we'll take you with us."

"Mr. Oliver won't, but Harry Martin might. I like him, Carey. Is everybody like him in Wybong?"

Carey had stood up and she bent over Tony and kissed his forehead.

"Nearly," she whispered, and she walked away along the veranda towards the steps.

Carey had the happiest morning she had had since she had first come to Two Creeks.

Harry said:

"There's room for Carey between us, isn't there, Mr. Reddin? We can't let the little lady reign it alone in the back and there's certainly not room there for my long legs."

Oliver gave Carey that strange intent glance of his.

"Is that all right with you, Carey? You will be comfortable enough?"

"Oh, yes," she said. "Then I can hear what you are both talking about."

"Of course you can," said Harry, as they got into the utility with Oliver at the steering-wheel. "After all, it's your farm, Carey girl."

When Harry spoke to her in this joking tender way Carey could see a small muscle in Oliver's cheek working. Perhaps he thought Harry was treating her like a child, too. Well, he wasn't. That was Harry's way. When she got the chance she would tell Oliver all about Harry. The trouble had been that neither Oliver nor any of the Reddin family had liked to hear about Wybong. She had felt so *silenced* about everything, and everybody, there.

All the same, as soon as the utility passed through the section of the fence that had been let down between Two Creeks and her own farm Oliver and Harry both seemed to forget they had a troublesome though necessary female with them. Oliver was full of detailed explanations and he answered all of Harry's questions easily and explicitly. Harry, too, when Oliver asked him what could be done about this and that, was very professional and explicit.

Listening to them both talking across her and over her head she suddenly felt lucky to have two such men taking her property in hand.

Quite unexpectedly she saw the wisdom of her father's choice of executor in his will. He had done the best for her, his only child. And she saw, too, the intended wisdom of Uncle Tam's trick in leaving her stranded on Oliver's hands. He had meant it for her own good. He had left her without any money so she couldn't run away. He had done it all for her sake, just as her father had done.

125

When they got back to the homestead Millicent and Jane had just got in from their ride. Millicent wore an old-fashioned black habit with a high white stock at her neck. Carey thought Millicent would always do things the way her grandparents did them. Jane was much more modern. She wore a beautiful pair of cream tailored jodhpurs with an open-necked white silk blouse into the neck of which was tucked a sky blue chiffon scarf. It was all a beautiful frame for her good figure and her pale smooth skin and gleaming red hair. They sat down in the cane chairs on the side veranda while Harry pulled up a chair for Carey and Oliver took the tray of drinks from Hannah.

"Now then, you two men," said Jane gaily. "Account for yourselves. Just what have you been finding in that rackety place over the way. Not a gold mine surely?"

"Potential," said Harry Martin easily. "Not the same kind of gold we have back home, eh, Carey?"

"It's not bedded in quartz and it's not yellow," laughed Carey. She had had a lovely morning with her two men and even Jane's magnificent appearance could not yet dampen her spirits.

"Don't tell me they have real gold in Wybong?" said Jane derisively.

"We've gold all right," Harry was answering Jane. "Gold, ilemite, magnesium and now uranium. . . ."

"Oh, really!" she said. "How marvellous. Why aren't they all millionaires back there?"

Carey touched Harry's foot with her own foot. He caught her eye and read in it that she did not wish him to dilate on Wybong. He rolled himself a cigarette and looked across the table at the beautiful supercilious creature on the other side.

"One day you come and see, Miss Newbold," he said. "Meantime let's talk about the weather. You ladies have a fine ride this morning?"

"Wonderful, thank you," said Millicent in her short clipped tones. "Carey, there was a delivery van from Melbourne this morning. Addressed to you. I can't imagine what's in it."

"Curtains," said Carey, taking her drink from Oliver.

Oliver looked at her, frowned as if trying to remember something and then the frown suddenly eased away and there was nearly a smile in his eyes. Carey, watching anxiously

126

that change in his expression, forgot for a moment there were others present.

Dear Oliver, she was thinking. *Please be pleased with me. They're my curtains, and I've had the courage to confront Millicent with them.*

Then she stopped thinking of Millicent and curtains and thought with a stab of realisation that she had . . . inside herself . . . addressed Oliver as *dear Oliver.* Why did it matter so very much to her?

" *Curtains!*" Millicent was saying. " What curtains? They weren't from the dry cleaners."

" No, they were from a Melbourne store," Carey said absently. " They're for the two end rooms. Mrs. Cleaver got them for me. Millicent, did Mrs. Cleaver ring up at all? I mean, I was half-expecting . . ."

" No, she didn't ring. At least, ask Hannah. I'm sure Hannah would have told me. I don't understand about the curtains. Those in the end rooms were perfectly good. . . ."

Dear Oliver. Why had she called him dear Oliver? How sweet it sounded, ringing there in the passages of her mind. If she looked at him now? But she dare not!

" I think curtains are a frightfully dull subject," said Jane. " I leave such deadly things to my housekeeper. What I really want to know is what you two men have been doing all the morning. You tell me, Oliver. I've an awful feeling that Mr. Martin is only going to tell me about Wybong."

" He has other resources of conversation, I assure you," said Oliver. He looked at Harry. " Jane doesn't like the subject of curtains, Mr. Martin. Shall we try her on water tables and land lifts and wind erosion?"

" I do not understand about the curtains," said Millicent persistently.

" Darling," said Jane, " we've got two perfectly good men between us. Let's make the most of them. Don't let us talk about things they couldn't possibly care about."

She tilted her head backwards over the head-rest and looked at Oliver with a pretended pout. He turned round at that moment. " Get me another drink, Oliver, would you?"

She really looked very beautiful lying back in the chair like that, the lines of her throat showing clear and smooth as she leaned her head back and half-turned it towards

Oliver. Her red hair swept backwards and fell in a luxuriant mass over the back of the chair. Her blouse was stretched neatly over her figure exaggerating its very good lines.

To take her glass from her hand Oliver had to lean over her.

Harry watched the scene through lazy eyes as if he was not really taking it in. Carey knew that far-away misleading look in Harry's eyes, and her heart dropped. A fool would not be taken in by what Jane was doing, and Harry was no fool.

"If you'll excuse me," Carey said, getting up, "I'll see if Tony has done his work and if he's been any trouble to Cook. Lunch will be ready in a minute, I expect. I'll ask Hannah . . ."

She tried hard not to run as she moved towards the door into the house. Once in the hall she almost fled towards the nether regions.

She spoke to Hannah first about lunch and to Cook next about whether Tony had been good or not. When she got to the back veranda Harry Martin was already there, sitting on Tony's bed examining a sheet of crayon drawings.

"Harry!" Carey said. "You're supposed to be at the second round of drinks. How did you get here?"

"I walked the long way round the veranda. When you left I left, too." He smiled. "The only lady I came down south to see was you, Carey girl. If you run away I have to run after you."

He put Tony's drawing down on the bed and stood up. Both of them had forgotten the small boy. He sat up on his pillows, a stick of yellow chalk twirling in his fingers and looked curiously from one face to the other.

"I didn't run away, Harry. I walked."

"You walked with your feet but you ran with your heart." He put his hands on her shoulders and faced her towards him. He shook his head slowly from side to side.

"Anything that's worth fighting for is worth staying for, love. I like your man, Carey. He's got quality. Stick to him. He won't let you down. . . ."

Suddenly Carey's shoulders drooped and in another minute Harry had his arms around her and her forehead rested on his shoulder.

"Oh, Harry! I didn't want to let you know. I wanted you to think I was so happy."

His big hand patted the back of her head.

"The way you flew into my arms down there on the railway line yesterday morning was like flying a red signal, love. The tears in your eyes and the tremble on your mouth were for someone who could give you a scrap of comfort." He put his hands on her shoulders and drew himself away from her. He looked down at her face. "I knew, Carey." he said. "You didn't have to tell me, and you didn't have to hide anything from me either."

He slipped his arm along Carey's shoulder.

"Let's go down the garden and talk about it," he said. "Let's think how we'd go about it way back in Wybong."

Together, Harry's arm still around Carey's shoulder, they walked down the steps, across the gravel path and into the garden.

Tony, his small brow thunderous, watched until the shrubs hid them from view. He hadn't understood the conversation; only that Harry had taken Carey in his arms and together they had walked away, his arm around her.

He stabbed the drawing-book in front of him with his coloured chalk. He drew a yellow heart and underneath, badly and angrily, he printed:

HARRY MARTIN LOVES CAREY
CAREY LOVES HARRY
I HATE THEM BOTH

Then with even greater fury he drew a cross across the page from corner to corner. He tore out the sheet screwed it up and threw it wildly across the floor.

Then he yelled.

"Hannah! Hannah! Hannah!"

Before Hannah could come running to his side he had thrown back the clothes and got out of bed. When Hannah arrived he was standing holding on to the bed rail with one hand and pressing the knee of his bandaged leg with the other.

"Heavens above!" cried Hannah. "What's the matter, Tony? I thought you were being killed."

"So I am, so I am, so I am," cried Tony in a rage. "I want to go back to Mrs. Wackett's. I hate being here. I hate everybody up here. . . ."

There was the sound of quick heavy footsteps coming around the veranda. Oliver turned the corner.

"What's going on here?" he demanded.

Carey came running through the shrubs in the garden and Jane and Millicent came around the corner of the veranda in Oliver's wake. Oliver took Tony by the shoulder and shook him slightly.

"What is the matter, young man?"

Jane stooped down and picked up the crumpled piece of paper from the floor. Tony made a dart at her, stumbled on his bad leg and would have fallen if Carey had not caught him.

"Tony . . . Tony, darling."

He buried his face in her skirt.

"It's your fault," he said. "It's all your fault."

He had snatched the paper from Jane and Oliver now took it out of his hand. Everyone, including Carey, was looking in bewilderment at Tony, as Oliver smoothed out the piece of paper. Harry Martin, coming up the veranda steps behind Oliver, glanced down at the printing on the paper and saw what it meant.

"Hannah . . . did something happen to him?" said Carey.

Jane sat down on Tony's bed, crossed her knees and leaned back on her hands.

"I hate to say it, Carey, but I think he's just having tantrums."

"Really, Oliver, that child does need disciplining . . ." began Millicent.

"No. No, he doesn't," said Carey, looking down and caressing Tony's head where he pressed it against her skirt. "Something has happened to upset him. Come on, Tony, you come up to my room with me. Do you think you could manage the staircase if I help you? If we wash your face and hands you'll feel better, then you can tell me all about it."

She took Tony's hand and turned away towards the door.

"You take his other hand, Hannah," she said. "I think we'll manage the stairs that way."

The three of them, Tony between, moved towards the door leading into the breakfast-room and thence to the cross passage and the hall.

Jane had put her hand in the pocket of her jodhpurs and brought out a cigarette-case and a lighter. She lit a cigarette.

"What is fascinating you about that piece of paper,

Oliver?" she asked. "Are you trying to interpret Tony's character from his scribbling?"

Harry moved back against the creepers; he leaned against the balustrade and watched Oliver's face.

With a sharp movement Oliver folded the paper across and then across again. He tore it into strips. His face was expressionless and his voice toneless.

"Shall we go and finish our drinks? I think we can leave Tony to Carey's ministrations."

"I'd better go and see Cook," said Millicent. "Now lunch will be at all hours." She hurried purposefully away.

Jane stood up.

"That's a splendid idea," said Jane. "Let's go and drown our sorrows if that little wretch of a Tony can't . . ."

Oliver turned to Harry, who had not said a word but who had watched each person out of his faded lazy eyes. He alone had noticed Oliver tear the paper into strips and put them in his inside pocket.

"Will you join us, Mr. Martin?" Oliver said carefully, quietly.

"Yes, I think I will," he drawled. "Can't let the whole party break up. You lead on, Mr. Reddin. I'll follow."

Upstairs in Carey's room some careful explanation was taking place.

"You see, Tony . . ." Carey was saying as she wiped the flannel over the small boy's face. He was sitting on the edge of her bed, his bandaged leg resting on the cover, the other leg dangling to the floor. "There are all sorts of ways of loving people. About six different kinds . . . like six different colours. Love is like a box of colours, in fact. I love you for one thing, which would mean I love you better than any other boy. I love Hannah which means I love her better than the people who helped in Mrs. Cleaver's house and at Cranston. I love Harry Martin because I never had a brother so I had him instead. And I never had a friend, a real friend that belonged to me, because I had to work so hard at Wybong I didn't have time to go out with the other boys and girls and have fun with them. So I love Harry like a brother; and instead of a friend."

Carey put the flannel down on the chair and picked up a towel and tenderly wiped Tony's face.

"I love Uncle Tam and it's quite different from the way I love you, or Hannah, or Harry Martin. . . ."

131

"Or Mr. Oliver?"

"Or Oliver," said Carey quietly.

"You love him?"

"Of course I do . . ." said Carey, folding the towel and walking to her dressing-table and taking a comb from the drawer. She came back to Tony and began to comb his hair. "One always loves one's husband, and that is quite another kind of love, too. Like red's different from blue, and yellow is different from white." Carey stood up straight. "Tony," she said severely, "do you love Mrs. Wackett?"

"Yes, I do."

"Do you love me?"

"Yes, I do."

"Is it the same as the way you love Mrs. Wackett?"

"No, it's not. You see, it's *different*. . . ."

Carey smiled.

"You see, don't you, Tony? It *is* different. But you can't quite say how, can you?"

"Well, it's different," said Tony. "Like white's different from yellow."

"Now you know. You've explained it to yourself. Tell me, do you want to go back to Mrs. Wackett now?"

"Not to-day, Carey, maybe I'll go back to-morrow. . . ."

"Okay. Well, you get into my bed and I'll have Hannah bring you up a tray. How's that for some spoiling?"

"Gee, Carey . . . I'd love that."

CHAPTER FOURTEEN

The fact that lunch passed off well was due to the well-bred manners of the Reddins and the anxiety of Carey not to let the troubles of the late morning show herself at too great a disadvantage in Harry's eyes as well as in Oliver's and Millicent's.

Though there was something remote and icy about Oliver, Carey had seen him so often like this that she could not detect from his manner just how angry he was, or otherwise, with Tony's hysterical performance.

Jane, she thought with relief, was involved more in conversational passes with Harry than with Oliver. She knew it was Harry's doing, and she was grateful to him.

After lunch, Millicent, now well inoculated in the theory she had to rest while at Two Creeks, insisted that Jane, too, must have a siesta.

They went up the staircase together and Carey was about to follow them as they all left the dining-room, when Harry called to her.

"Carey," he said, "I want to talk to Mr. Reddin for half an hour about that farm. You'd better sit in." He turned to Oliver. "I've been thinking. I've got a pretty good idea of the set-up. What I need now is to get together a team of men, lay out some plans and offer you a tender for the contract. Right?"

"Yes," said Oliver. "Shall we go into my study or do you prefer the veranda?"

"The veranda, hey Carey? We can look at the scenery as well." He laughed his easy fresh laugh.

"Very well," said Oliver. "I expect we can ask Hannah to make us some more coffee."

"I'll tell her now, Oliver," Carey said. "You go on, will you?"

She didn't feel in any hurry to join the men. So much had happened in the morning, ranging from happiness when she had been out with Oliver and Harry to the depths of unhappiness when Jane had staged her act on the veranda. Between the two extremes had been her breakdown with Harry when she had realised that his shrewd eyes had missed nothing of the hollowness of her marriage with Oliver Reddin; her real concern for Tony . . . and always the hankering, like a persistent relentless ache, to be alone with Oliver, to try to find some point at which he would unbend.

Harry and Oliver had both taken chairs by the round table on the veranda. They sat at a slight angle to one another so they both could look out over the garden and the paddocks beyond. Oliver meticulously offered Harry a cigarette. Harry took it and was quick to take his matches from his pocket and light Oliver's cigarette first, then his own.

"He's a handsome devil . . . used to his own way," Harry thought. "And a will of iron. A tough man to fight, but might make a good friend."

Oliver addressed his attention to the paddocks beyond the garden fence. As they had taken their places they had been talking about the Melbourne Cup which was in the not far distant future.

133

"There are four Two Creeks horses running in one race or another on Cup Day," Oliver said. "You'd better come down and look at their dams before you leave us, Mr. Martin."

"I'd like to look at your stock altogether, Mr. Reddin. I know it's pretty famous stuff, but I wouldn't like you to catch me out on breeding. You're the master on the race-horse class."

"It's my business," said Oliver. "And it was my father's business before me. Learned a great deal from Reg Fraser in my youth."

"You'll outclass me there," said Harry in his slow drawl. "But you won't outclass me on a good mountain breed. A horse that is man's friend in the outback . . . that is, will carry any stockman anywhere any time of the year. I think I'd pick 'em better than you would."

Oliver stiffened imperceptibly. He would tell breeding and quality in a horse anywhere in the world, and he knew it. Harry Martin, a surveyor and road contractor, was challenging him on his own ground.

"I think I could pick quality in a horse whether he was race-course or station bred," Oliver said quietly.

"I'll make you a bet," said Harry. "You a betting man, Mr. Reddin? "

"I bet heavily on the Melbourne Cup," Oliver said dryly. "I don't know an Australian who doesn't."

"The stakes won't be money for this one," said Harry. "It will be something else."

Oliver turned his head and looked at Harry Martin. Carey, coming to the veranda, could feel the electricity between the two men. They rose simultaneously as Carey took a chair on the other side of Oliver, across the table from Harry.

"Hannah's coming," she said.

But Oliver and Harry were still standing looking straight and hard at one another.

"Sit down, Mr. Martin," Oliver said almost peremptorily.

"Yes thanks, I will," Harry said, and he sat down. He smiled across the table at Carey. Then he glanced back at Oliver.

"I'm going to bet you, Mr. Reddin, that if you come in to Preston and look at those three horses I brought down from Wybong . . . now in Smithson's grazing paddock . . .

they're as good a quality, in their class, as your horses down there on your track are in their class."

"Harry . . ." said Carey.

He made a gesture with his hand to silence her. Oliver did not move.

"There can never be any comparison between an un-pedigreed horse and a thoroughbred," he said.

"You're right," said Harry. "But first you got to 'make the mental leap that'll take you into the class that isn't thoroughbred. The class that's just tough mountain bred. Then you look at those horses in their own right . . . not in any other horse's right."

"I think your premises are absurd, Mr. Martin," Oliver said quietly. "But I'll take your bet. If I think your horses are as good a quality in their class as mine are in the thoroughbred class I'm to admit it? Right?"

"Right," said Harry.

"And what then?" said Oliver. "I accept them and run them on Carey's farm? Is that what this is all about, Mr. Martin?"

"No," said Harry. "If you want them you can have them. If you don't I'll take 'em home, *whatever* your decision."

"You realise that I only have to give my decision, and there is no court of appeal?"

"Yes, I do. You're too good a horse man, Mr. Reddin, to barter your immortal soul for a lie. If you think those horses are as good in their class as your horses are in their class . . . you'll say so."

"Thank you," said Oliver briefly. "And the stake?"

"We're coming to that," drawled Harry. He let a minute's silence hang on the air. "I say my horses are as good as yours . . . in their class. And you make the decision. If I'm right I take Carey home to Wybong with me three days hence. I can do the initial planning of my business down here in three days, rising at cock crow."

There was a complete silence on the veranda. Nothing moved, not even the spirals of smoke that refused to waft away from the cigarettes on the still warm air. It was Carey who broke it.

"But Harry . . ." she said. "Two Creeks is my home now. I *have* to stay here. You didn't ask *me* about your bet. . . ."

"I didn't have to, Carey. I knew you'd come for another

135

reason. I didn't spoil the day for you yesterday by telling you the news from Wybong. Your old Uncle Tam's not too good. He's had a bout of 'flu and it's knocked his heart."

"Harry!" almost wailed Carey. "Why didn't you tell me? How bad is he?"

"Not too bad, Carey girl, else I'd have had to tell you. All the same I guess you'll come back with me if I ask you."

"Oh yes. . . ." Then she stopped short and looked at Oliver.

Oliver was looking straight ahead of him. Her eyes clouded. She looked quickly back at Harry.

"But that is an unfair bet," she said. "If Oliver doesn't like the horses and says so it will look as if he is stopping me going. . . ."

"Not if I know Mr. Reddin," said Harry.

Oliver glanced across at him.

"You are quite right," he said. "I do not make mis-statements on horses for ulterior motives. I think your bet is a slightly fantastic one, Mr. Martin, but as you are my guest and as you have requested it, I will accept the challenge. Since you have gone to the trouble, and the expense, of bringing those horses to Preston I will at least pay you the courtesy of looking at them."

"Thank you," said Harry amiably. "Let's drink to that in coffee."

Oliver stood up.

"We can begin by your coming down and looking at my thoroughbreds," he said. "Maybe it will be you, Mr. Martin, who will change your mind."

"Maybe I will," said Harry affably. "And if that's the case I'll say so." He had risen as he spoke and the two men walked to the edge of the veranda.

"I'll get one of the men to bring the utility round," Oliver said, and he went rapidly down the three steps and along the path by the side of the house that led to the homestead garages. He did not once look at Carey.

She stood up and went to Harry's side.

"What can I do?" she said, looking at him with anxiety. "I want to see how Uncle Tam is. But I don't want to go away from Two Creeks just now. You see . . . I have visitors. There's Jane here . . ." She quickly added "and Millicent" because she was ashamed of letting Harry know

136

how much she hated to leave Jane alone in the homestead with Oliver. Jane would spend the whole time twisting back her head so that her red hair would hang down in that beguiling way.

"You won't have to make the choice, Carey girl," said Harry. "It all rests on a bet. The choice will be your husband's."

"But what if I don't agree?"

"You'll do as he tells you, Carey. You'll come home to Wybong with me. Because that's what I think his judgment will be."

"Oh, Harry . . . are you two making decisions about me or about horses?"

"Both."

Carey looked out over the garden.

If Oliver wants me, Carey thought, *all he's got to do is reject Harry's horses. He's only got to say so. . . .*

Then in a sudden panic she thought she saw what Harry's motives were. He was asking Oliver to make the decision as to whether he really valued this seemingly phoney marriage or was prepared to send Carey back from whence she came.

Her heart smarted sorely at the humiliation of Harry *knowing.* Yet she knew Harry loved her. Whatever he was doing would be out of kindness.

Harry and Oliver drove into Preston and Harry sat on the step of the utility and rolled himself one cigarette after another while Oliver stood at the fence rail and looked over the brumbies. Harry looked up once. It was when Oliver entered the paddock and quietly and expertly cornered one of the horses, made it come to him by sheer force of will power, and then carefully and slowly looked over its points.

After Oliver had done this with each animal and had spent a long time looking in their eyes, their mouths, and running his hands over them he came back to the fence and stood and watched them in silence.

"What's he doin'?" Smithson, who was sitting in the utility, asked Harry.

"I'd say, at this stage he's lost a bet. He doesn't want to lose it. A man like Mr. Reddin doesn't want to admit anything but a thoroughbred is as first-class horse."

Oliver walked back to the utility.

137

"You win, Mr. Martin," he said without emotion. "I'll take those three horses and run them on Carey's farm. Smithson can take them out for me."

Smithson started up the engine of the utility with a roar.

"And I take Carey home with me?" Harry asked, rolling himself yet another cigarette but not looking up.

Still Oliver showed no emotion.

"Yes. I presume she wants to go."

"Her uncle's a sick man. And an old one," Harry said smoothly, as he tucked the tobacco into the end of the paper roll with a match stick.

"You can lay your plans for the farm inside three days? I presume you will collect your team of men elsewhere and send them down? When do you propose to be back?"

"About three weeks' time should be soon enough."

Harry was now smoking his cigarette and he looked at Oliver through lazy innocent eyes.

"I'm not saying Carey will come back with me though. When she gets home to Wybong she might find she's needed there. She might stay awhile. It's up to her. That okay?"

He saw the line of Oliver's mouth tighten but otherwise there was no expression in his face. His eyes were icy cold and impersonal.

"Carey makes her own decisions," Oliver said.

The two men got into the utility with Smithson and drove back to the agency.

Carey, when she heard the verdict, was bewildered. All the joy she might have felt in having Oliver accept the brumbies was lost in her dismay that he showed no feeling at all about her proposed return to Wybong with Harry. He had gone about dealing with that matter in exactly the same manner as he had gone about arranging for her to go to Mrs. Cleaver and later marry himself. The only relief in what was now a sombre world for Carey was the fact that Jane had already announced she was going to Sydney for a long-booked bridge party.

"I believe I'll come back to Victoria via Wybong," she said to Harry Martin. "Who knows . . . I just might find it quite the heaven you two think it is."

She now referred to Harry and Carey as "you two" and Carey had the sore misgiving that Jane's sudden interest in Wybong was in order to see for herself if there was anything in this "relationship" between Carey and Harry.

At least she was removing that glorious hair and that tantalising figure from the Two Creeks dining-table for some part of Carey's absence.

On the day Oliver drove them into Preston to catch the train to Albury she felt that the homestead of Two Creeks might never have known her.

She felt as she had on her wedding night when she had waited alone in that bedroom for Oliver to join her. She wanted to do the right thing, and do it easily and naturally, without coyness on the one hand or clumsiness on the other. The very anxiety of it, in anticipation, made her as nervous as she had been on that wedding night.

She was a little distressed at parting from Tony.

"I'll be back," she said. "I'll be back." Then she wondered if she really would; if Oliver would want her back. At all events she would one day be back on her own farm. She and Tony would be togethe again.

Millicent had frozen up at the news that Carey was going back to Wybong with Harry Martin. The oddest thing about Millicent was that she had a hurt look in her eyes, as if someone had done her personal grievous harm. She had it there when she looked at Harry Martin. Carey thought it might be because Millicent considered it had all been Harry's idea with that "bet" of his. Of course it had far more to do with the fact that Uncle Tam was ill, as far as Carey was concerned.

It puzzled Carey for she had quite expected Millicent's only reaction to be:

"What do you expect of a child like Carey? Of course she would give in to the temptation to go running home at the slightest provocation."

CHAPTER FIFTEEN

Jane was to leave for Sydney in her own car two hours before Carey and Harry were to leave for Wybong.

Earlier they were having afternoon tea on the veranda and Millicent had risen to carry Oliver's tea to him in the study.

"Oh, Carey," Jane laughed, "after five hours alone in the train with Harry, however will you fill in the five hours' wait at Albury for the Western Mail? In the small hours of the morning, too! Oh, well, even on the border the stars shine. There's nothing like counting stars in good company to induce sleep."

"There is an excellent waiting-room and restaurant at Albury," Millicent said with some asperity, as she turned away, with the cup and saucer in her hand. "I had a long wait there once myself. . . ."

"And I suppose you can snatch an hour or two's sleep before getting there," said Jane. "Harry! Have you got a soft shoulder as well as a good broad one?"

"Carey can have a loan of my shoulder any time she likes," Harry said, with a lazy smile. "That goes for you, too, Miss Jane, when you come up Wybong way."

Millicent had reached the door and was about to go into the house. Harry's eyes followed her.

"And if Miss Millicent would come along, too, she could have both of 'em . . . she'd be that welcome," he said.

By the drawling way Harry said those words Carey knew he meant them. Dear Harry . . . she thought. She hoped that Millicent, stiff and proper though she was, would understand that anyone in the world would find safety on Harry's shoulder. He was not being brash. He was being his honest, utterly reliable, self.

Millicent hesitated for the fraction of a minute.

"Thank you," she said. She did not turn round but went through the door. The "thank you" was muffled and soft but Carey did not think that Millicent sounded offended. Her dignity had not been affronted by that kindly offer. The thing that had most surprised Carey was that Millicent had been visibly upset about her, Carey's, return to Wybong. She had thought that Millicent would be pleased to have Two Creeks to herself again.

Oliver drove the big car into the station yard at Preston a few minutes before the train was due in.

The train puffed in leisurely as if tired enough to be glad of the ten-minute wait while stock trucks were shunted off on to the side lines.

Oliver bought some fruit and chocolates and stowed them on the rack in the compartment. He exchanged a few words of desultory conversation with Harry on the subject of

140

the gang of men to come on to Carey's farm for the fencing.

With her heart dropping lower and lower Carey thought he would keep this up even after they got into the train and it began to pull out.

It was Harry who tactfully broke away.

"I'm going down to see what the dining-car is like, Carey girl, and what sort of a meal we're likely to expect. I'll get on board down there and see you later."

He shook hands with Oliver. Carey did not hear what they said in this brief farewell because she was watching Oliver's face. She could do that now that he wasn't looking at her.

When Harry turned away Oliver turned to Carey.

She knew then she need not have worried about last awkward farewells. There weren't going to be any farewells. Oliver would shake hands with her in the same impersonal way as he had shaken hands with Harry.

Pain vied with disappointment and in some oblique way she wanted to punish Oliver who so hurt her.

She let her eyes drop down to her hands in that old trick of hers and then she looked up again at Oliver. Unconsciously she hoped this would do something to dent the armour of his aloofness.

His grey eyes . . . with the little black line around the iris . . . flashed a spark of anger. Carey thought he might really, actually, smack her, as once he had promised to do if she dropped her eyes like that again.

She lifted her round chin and looked at him through a pair of steady blue eyes.

"Good-bye, Oliver," she said, with a stiff little smile. "Do you know what the stockmen outback say when they're going away and might or might not come that way again? The say . . . '*Cheerio! I'll see you somehow, some place, some day.*'"

She held out her hand and Oliver, taking off his hat with his left hand, took her hand with his right hand.

For a minute it seemed as if he was not going to release it. His eyes lost the distant impersonal expression and were looking at her as if he was really seeing her . . . seeing into her.

Carey, with her head high, withdrew her hand. It was too late for Oliver to *see* her now . . . to look at her as if he wanted to know what kind of a person she was under

141

that earnest smile. He should have done that on the 18th October, her wedding day. She hadn't known until this minute how bitter disappointment could be.

But her smile did not waver.

"It was nice being married to you," she said. "And I loved Two Creeks." She turned and walked quickly towards the entrance to the compartment. She did not look back and once inside the doorway of the carriage she stood in the corridor, her back to the panelling of the compartments, and facing the window that looked out on the other side from the station over paddocks running over limitless distances towards the western horizon.

Behind her, on the platform, Oliver would be standing —or going—she did not know which. She no longer wished to know. She leaned against the panelling and closed her eyes. She braced herself as the train shuddered into movement, and stayed there until it had slid out of the railway yards and out into the country. Then she went to her compartment and sat down.

"No tears," she said. "No beastly, beastly tears!" But in spite of her brave words they stung in her eyes and then one by one toppled over and ran down her cheeks.

It was ten minutes before Harry Martin joined her.

"Why so sombre?" he asked as he settled her magazines and his own books beside their seats and then sat down in the corner seat facing her.

"Why do you think, Harry?"

He did not answer but looked at her quietly and gravely, so she went on:

"Why have you done this, Harry? It wasn't only because Uncle Tam was sick, was it?"

"No, Carey girl, it wasn't." He took out his packet of tobacco and began to roll himself a cigarette.

"Then why?" asked Carey again.

"I like your man, Carey. I told you that once before. I like Oliver Reddin. He's a man any other man would have a lot of respect for. I think maybe he's a bit hard round the region of the heart." He looked up quickly then went on with the business of making a cigarette.

"I like my Carey, too. She's a girl that needs a lot of love. You know, like a hot-house plant needs warmth and water. So I reckoned I'd take you back to Wybong where you'd get plenty of that."

"Oliver never shows his feelings," Carey said. "Supposing

142

inside he does love me. . . ." Wishful thinking, but she had to say it. Anyhow it was too late now . . . after what *she* had said.

"In that case," said Harry, poking the tobacco into its cover with a match stick, "he'll come after you."

The last words startled Carey. There was a long silence.

"Supposing he doesn't come after me? They're very proud, the Reddins. . . ."

"Then they can keep their pride in splendid solitude and we'll keep you. You'll get over it, Carey. People always do. Funny, but love is the most fickle of all the emotions. You take *friendship* now. Just plain, everyday, backyard friendship. . . ."

"Supposing he does come?"

"He can have you back if he comes because he loves you. If it's to save that Reddin pride, old Harry Martin will soon know. I can pick pride as quick as I can pick a good brumby, and Oliver Reddin can pick a thoroughbred."

"Harry," Carey asked quietly. "Why is everybody running my life now? Uncle Tam . . . when he left me at Two Creeks. Oliver. You . . ."

"Well, love," he said, with a quiet smile, "sooner or later there had to be a reckoning. We let you run us all, back there at Wybong, but that was really because men like to have a pretty girl managing them. Specially when she did it in the artful-artless way Carey Fraser did it. She had to learn some day she could only rule her kingdom up there in Wybong because her subjects let her rule it. And because they liked it. Sooner or later she had to find out that underneath they were running her. You see, it suited everyone to have things ship-shape, and Carey Fraser was the one to do it . . . because she was so sweet and lovable about it."

Harry turned and shed a little ash in the ash-tray on the arm rest of his seat.

"Things weren't panning out too well for Carey down there at Two Creeks. So we had to come out in our true colours. We had to come and do a little running of Carey in the open."

"We?" asked Carey in a subdued voice.

"Uncle Tam and I. Uncle Tam first. 'Get down there to Two Creeks, Harry, and see how things are going with my lass. If she's good and happy put in a gang to clean up that farm for her and let her be. If she's not . . . bring her home'."

" Then he's not sick at all?"

" Well . . . he told me he was. You know what Uncle Tam is, Carey. Maybe he was and maybe he wasn't. He was never one for doing things the direct way."

Harry grinned, then went on :

" Who am I to question a good honest man so much older than myself, and whose motives towards his niece were of the very highest order?"

Carey's back stiffened.

" Harry! You deceived me. You know I would never have come if I hadn't thought Uncle Tam was sick, and needed me."

" Wouldn't you, Carey?" he said quietly. " Sooner or later . . . wouldn't you have come home?"

At Two Creeks, dinner over, Millicent sat in one of the small arm-chairs of Oliver's study and read the mail while Oliver went through some accounts at his desk.

" You would have a better light if you went into the drawing-room, Millicent," Oliver said without looking up.

" It's too quiet in the drawing-room," Millicent replied. " There's more company here."

Oliver looked up then and Millicent met his eyes.

" You shouldn't have let her go," Millicent said with sudden vehemence. " What do you suppose people will say? You should be President of the Shire Council un-opposed. People expect it. What will they think about your wife going away like that before they've even met her? You need her, and the whole Shire needs her. They expect the president's wife to play a part. . . ."

" That had nothing to do with feeling lonely sitting in the drawing-room by yourself. You have been doing that for much of your lifetime," Oliver interrupted abruptly.

Millicent moved her position in her chair with a gesture of irritation.

" Well, after a house party things are always a little dull."

" You used to be pleased when people went home so that you could have a rest . . . and put the homestead in order again."

Millicent stiffened and assumed an expression of pained patience.

" I don't wish to have an argument with you, my dear brother. You should not have let her go. That is my last word ; except to say that I'm very surprised at a man like Harry Martin placing Carey in such an ambiguous situation."

"So you didn't find him so hard to accept, after all?"

Millicent flushed, a very unusual demonstration of feelings for her.

"My opinions do not matter with you these days, Oliver. What does matter is the good name of the Reddins. It is outrageous to think your wife appears to have so little interest in the affairs of the Shire that she goes away at a crucial time, even before people in the district have had time to call on her." She paused. Then she went on: "Furthermore, there will be no one here to receive your guests at the gymkhana and the polo season. . . ." Millicent took in a deep breath. She changed her tone somewhat before she added: "Carey is much more capable than I guessed at first. She could have managed the duties very well. Her manner is very good. Quite charming, in fact."

Oliver appeared to go on with his work and did not answer. Millicent made a half-angry, half-exasperated movement as she gathered together her letters, some of which were on her lap and some on the small table beside her.

"I have an urge to see this Wybong myself," she said at length. "If Jane can afford to satisfy her curiosity, so can I. Furthermore, any visit I might pay there would serve to mitigate against gossip that might arise from Carey leaving her home with——" Millicent's voice faltered— "with Harry Martin," she said. She had gathered her mail into one hand now and she stood up. "I'm going to my room," she added. "You are no company, Oliver. You live the life of a judge . . . sittting there behind your table. And I'm afraid your judgment is academic and has no relation to the realities of life. You deal in problems and not in people."

She walked slowly to the door as if hoping that Oliver would say something. At the door she turned and opened her mouth as if to make one last sally. When she saw her brother's face she stopped.

"I'm half inclined to go with you myself," he said quietly. He paused, then added, "I also would like to see this . . . Wybong."

"To see Wybong, and not Carey?" asked Millicent curiously.

"I would like to see just exactly what it is in Wybong that so attracts Carey. Other than Harry Martin, of course."

He noticed that Millicent winced.

Yes, it was the kind of blow at Reddin pride he should not let pass. He understood Millicent's feelings. He passed his hand over his face as if suddenly tired.

"I feel as if I have been in some kind of a daze; as if I have not been seeing clearly." He stood up abruptly. "You are quite right, Millicent. It was extremely bad judgment on my part allowing Carey to go . . . without me. I can't understand myself. I don't like to be found at fault in matters of judgment. I have a certain pride in being accurate in my summing up of situations. I could have given an honest opinion about those horses, and then gone to Wybong with them."

Millicent already had her free hand on the door. She looked at her brother in surprise.

"You actually think you were wrong in letting them go . . . like that?"

There was an expression in Oliver's eyes that inexplicably touched Millicent's heart.

"As you have said, Millicent, I am an academic judge of people, and not a practical one. I spend too much time examining facts, and not the motives. . . ."

"You think people might *talk*?" Millicent asked uneasily as if Oliver thinking this gave much more cause for alarm than if she thought it herself.

He lifted his hands in a gesture then let them fall to his side.

"That is beside the point," he said with a touch of his old reserve. "We will leave in the morning. We will overland by car. Will you let Hannah and Cook know? And telephone to see that Mother will be all right for another week?"

Millicent was so relieved she suddenly looked ten years younger.

"It's a long way. We'd better leave early. It might take us three days if the roads are bad. I'd better find out about hotels." Both her voice and step lightened as she went through the door.

Oliver listened to her receding footsteps and then sat down again. His pen traced small patterns on the blotter in front of him, his mouth had the drawn white line around it, and the small muscle worked in his cheek.

As Millicent had said . . . the house echoed an accusing silence around him. Yet in every room, in the hall and passages, there was a flitting ghost of a young girl who always smiled. Around her was an aura of happiness, of sound and laughter.

He was very alone in the silence of his study.

CHAPTER SIXTEEN

It was late afternoon, an hour before sundown when Oliver drove the big overlanding car into Wybong.

For quite a long time he and Millicent had been silent. They hadn't known there would be bitumen all the way to Wybong. Oliver's road map was three years old and it showed a gravel track for a hundred miles west of the dust bowl. They had expected at least another day on the road.

In the commercial room of the hotel in which they had stayed last night he had seen a recent pastoral map tacked to the wall. It showed Wybong in heavy black type.

He turned to an agent who was sitting at a table making out his day's orders.

"Since when?" Oliver asked, putting his finger under Wybong.

The man looked up.

"Oh, since uranium and oil joined the gold in the district outback of the town," he replied. "'Bout three years, I think." The man grinned. "Suppose you thought the world ended at the Victoria border, hey?"

The bitumen highway ran right through Wybong, cutting it in half as neatly as a bisected circle.

Civilisation after eighty miles of bush scrub began with some old shanties, then shortly changed to wood and iron bungalows resplendent in modern paints and begirdled with shrub gardens.

"Must be water here," said Millicent. "Those gardens . . ."

"Outback towns always rise on water-holes or a permanent creek bed," Oliver said shortly.

"Good heavens," said Millicent. "Look at those buildings. And the shops. *Very modern.*"

Oliver said nothing.

"We've passed one hotel. Quite pleasant and new, it looked. I suppose it is better to stop at one nearer the centre of the town? Oliver, what do you suppose *that*

147

place is? It's more imposing than our own Shire offices."

" The carving over the doorway says ' Public Library '."

" In the middle of the desert! Good gracious me!"

" I imagine that very big modern building on the rise on the hill over there is the high school," said Oliver dryly.

" But we haven't even got one in Preston."

" Perhaps I'd better do something about catching up with Wybong when I'm in office," Oliver said.

There was a curious note in his voice and Millicent looked at him sideways.

Her brother was smiling . . . actually smiling.

Millicent swallowed. Well, of course, if she had been wrong she would be the first to admit it.

Oliver swung his car to the side of the road and parked it alongside the kerb. He judged he was dead centre of the town and the hotel on the left looked a good one.

He got out of the car, walked round and opened the door for Millicent and then took their two cases from the back. He followed Millicent into the lobby of the hotel.

The farther north they had driven the hotter it had become. Two hundred miles back Oliver had taken off his coat and thrown it on to the back seat. He left it there. He could see and feel he wasn't going to need any coat in Wybong.

As they entered the hotel they walked into a cool draught of air.

" Air conditioned!" said Millicent, startled.

" Seems like it," said Oliver. He nodded to a desk partially hidden by an array of palms. " I think we register over there."

He put the cases down and walked towards the desk. A middle-aged man greeted him with a pleasant smile.

" Can I do anything for you, sir?"

" I'd like two rooms, one for my sister and one for myself. We haven't booked. . . ."

" That's all right, sir. We accommodate through travellers. Would you please sign the register."

He turned away to take two keys from the rack. When he turned back he swung the register round and quickly read the signature there.

" Your cases will be taken through for you, Mr. Reddin," he said smoothly. " Your rooms face the south and will be cooler. There's hot and cold water . . . Say!" He stopped

148

and looked at Oliver with greater interest. "I've heard that name before. You been here before, sir? No! By crikey . . . that's the name young Carey Fraser married. You wouldn't be related? To a girl in our town, sir?"

"The same family," said Oliver. "Did you say there was hot and cold water in the room? If my sister goes to her room now is it possible for her to get some tea?"

"Certainly, sir. Room service any hour of the day or night." He leaned round Oliver to speak to Millicent. "Just lift your bedside telephone, miss. Order anything you like. That is, unless you'd like to go to the Espresso lounge. Through that glass door, right of the dining-room." He turned back to Oliver. "Very pleased to have you with us, sir. Anyone related to Carey Fraser is always welcome in this town."

"You know her?" asked Millicent as if she had to ask the question and could only just bring herself to do so.

"Know her? I'll say I do. Carey does the flowers when the Rotary Club or Legacy or the Returned Soldiers have their big dinners here. They reckon they wouldn't have any dinner if Carey didn't do the decoration." He broke off and gave a lugubrious smile. "That is until she went away and married into your family, miss. Your gain's our loss I can tell you . . ."

"How do you grow flowers in this climate?" asked Millicent disbelievingly.

"All the big stations have got gardens. Shade-houses, too. Down round the Olympic swimming-pool there's big gardens and shade-houses. We're never without flowers in Wybong." Would you like some tea right away, sir?"

"No thank you," Oliver said shortly. "I'm going out. Millicent, you would probably like to remove some of the travel stains and have a rest. I will see you later."

"All right, Oliver. Don't hurry back."

Millicent turned to follow her case now being carried by a porter and Oliver went through the main entrance again.

Out in the street he stopped and looked up and down its length. There were several big cars outside the stores. An ancient spring-cart drawn by a dapper young mare rattled past. A young girl and boy went past on horses and a minute later an outsize station-wagon purred along resplendent in blue enamel and chrome fittings.

The men in the street ranged from some bow-legged stockmen weathered an earth brown by a lifetime exposed to sun and wind to some extremely well-dressed men, all coatless but wearing spotless long-sleeved white shirts with reticent ties.

"The business executives," Oliver thought, summing them up.

The women were hatless, wore attractive sun-dresses showing bared neck and arms.

"Gold gipsy ear-rings are all the go in Wybong apparently," thought Oliver.

He crossed the street and walked a hundred yards until he came to a tea-shop.

Inside it was cool, and almost empty. Rather a late hour for afternoon tea to attract the citizens, he thought. He sat down at a table and when a waitress came to him he ordered tea and sandwiches.

"You a stranger here?" the girl asked when she came back with her tray. She was slim, dark-haired, with curious but friendly eyes.

"Yes," Oliver said. "Do you know whereabouts a Mr. Tam Fraser lives in Wybong?"

"Certainly I do," the girl replied as she deftly set the table with a mat, plate and knife and began to dispose the teapot, milk and sugar in a semi-circle around them. "Everyone knows old Tam Fraser. Owns a place called Stockmen's Rest right at the top end of the street. Turn left when you go out. Last place in town. Can't miss it because there's a big pepper tree over the gate and you'll see the stockmen sitting about under the trees. There's a whole gang in town right now from Cartheroo station. Old Mr. Tam lives at the pub opposite these days but now Carey's home he's back at the old homestead."

"You know Carey Fraser?"

"That's not her name now. She got married. Some fellow down south. Rich, they say. But Carey wouldn't marry him for *that*. Everyone in town knows her, and out at the big stations, too. Real smiler, she is, with a way of her own. Look, sir. See through that window? That's the hospital. Carey raised all the money for that. Two little wood and iron shanties we used to have and when they discovered uranium and oil at Cartheroo they knew this town'd boom and they'd have to have a decent hospital. Harry Martin . . . he's the boss cocky in this town . . . got Carey Fraser to collect

150

the money because he knew everyone'd give to her. So they did. And so they ought to. What she did helping up at that hospital when they were short staffed is just nobody's business. Awful good with children, is Carey. How she bothers with them I don't know. My dad reckons children are the best judge of human beings. They can always tell the dinkum* from the phoney. Anyhow they liked Carey all right. Do anything for her. Like the stockmen down at The Rest. Well, as I was saying . . . Oh, excuse me, sir. There's another customer in. At this hour, too!"

She sped away to lighten another's tea hour with her news of the day.

Oliver drank his tea and ate one sandwich. Then as he went to the counter to pay his bill the waitress hastened to speed him on his way.

"Right down the street, sir, if you're looking for Mr. Tam. Keep going till you come to the end of the town."

Oliver thanked her politely and went out.

He walked about four hundred yards until he came to a tobacconist's shop. He went in and asked for some cigarettes.

"Am I going in the right direction for Mr. Tam Fraser's house?" he asked a dark sleek-haired man serving him.

"Right on to the end, sir. You looking for Mr. Tam? You'll find him at his old homestead. Now Carey's home. . . ."

Oliver flicked an eyebrow.

"You know Carey?" he said curiously. "Everyone in this town knows Carey."

The man grinned.

"Of course we do. Best-liked girl in Wybong. And prettiest, too. When they opened the Olympic pool she won the bathing beauty competition hands down."

"She won the *what*?" said Oliver. "Do you mean to tell me she got up in a swim-suit with the whole town looking at her. . . ."

"Now look, mister . . . don't you get that wrong. This is a very respectable town and Carey Fraser might look a bobby-dazzler in a swim-suit but there's nobody north of the border would say a word about her except she's the nicest girl in town. The station owner's daughters were in that competition too. It was to raise money for the hospital."

Oliver noticed that the sleek-haired young man in the
* Real.

151

white barber's coat and with the thin delicate white hands looked as if he might wax a little belligerent on the subject of Carey Fraser being a nice girl.

"That's all right with me," said Oliver. "I just happen to be related to her."

Fire died in the young man.

"Well, sorry sir, if you got me wrong."

"I didn't. I got you very right."

Oliver went to the door. He turned and grinned at the man.

"I'll tell Carey your high opinion of her."

He went out, turned left and came face to face with Harry Martin.

There was a moment's silence and then both men put out their hands. Harry grinned as he shook hands with Oliver.

"Had a feeling you wouldn't spare Carey too long," he said. "I was looking for you. I saw your car outside the hotel and Bill Brown at the desk told me you'd gone out and that you had Miss Reddin with you. She was in her room but I didn't visit her. I thought I'd come and find you first."

"That's good of you, but I'm sure she would have been pleased to see you. I hear you're something called 'the boss cocky of this town'."

"Well, Shire President . . . and I guess you know what that means," Harry said, with a grin. "I believe you're all set to be Shire President down there at Preston yourself."

He took out his tobacco and began to roll a cigarette. The two men moved to the side of the pavement to let a woman and a pram go by.

"Well, that's what I wanted to see you about," Harry went on, watching his own fingers deftly roll the tobacco in its paper shell. "And I wanted your permission to pay my respects to Miss Millicent."

Oliver looked at Harry in astonishment.

"Do they do things as properly as that in Wybong?" he asked. He took out a cigarette and proceeded to light it.

"Well, not altogether. I just happen to like Miss . . . Millicent. You know what, Mr. Reddin, she's a bit old-fashioned herself, and I rather kinda like it." He looked up. "Let's put it this way." He suddenly grinned. "She

152

reminds me of my mother . . . and I was very fond of my mother. I guess she was like Millicent when she was young. Very good at running committees in the Shire . . . that sort of thing."

Oliver noticed the " Miss " had been dropped altogether now.

" Well, look, Mr. Martin," he said. " I think you'd better go along and tell her so yourself. . . ."

" As long as I've got your okay. And my name's Harry, by the way." He looked up from lighting his cigarette. " What do you think . . . Oliver?" he asked, looking straight into Oliver's eyes.

Oliver hesitated, then suddenly his face relaxed into a smile.

" Where can I find Carey, Harry?" he asked.

" Right on to the end of the town. She's there. Bossing those stockmen about like nobody's business. Well, I'll be seeing you later, Oliver. Maybe we can have dinner together. All of us."

" Maybe," said Oliver.

Perplexed, he watched Harry Martin walking composedly away towards the hotel. He turned and went on down the main street.

At the Stockmen's Rest Oliver saw two wizened horny-handed stockmen talking over the fence by the pepper tree that guarded the path leading to an old sprawling homestead.

" Good day, mate," they both said as Oliver entered the gate.

" Good day," Oliver replied and nodded his head. They went on with their conversation and paid no further attention to him.

It was clear the well-trodden path led along the side of the house and past a wide veranda.

As he reached the corner of the homestead where he could see into the kitchen he could see a figure, very much enveloped in a white apron and with a scarf tied mammy-fashion round her head, busying herself at a big table in the centre of the room. He knew it was Carey.

He stopped and turned and looked down to the paddock, beyond the yard, that lay on his left. There were several sheds sprouting out like disconnected wings from the house on that side and in the shadow of them were a number of stockmen, sitting on a wooden bench, polishing harness.

Across the path from them was a very big, very old gum tree.

Oliver turned away from the homestead and walked down the path to the gum tree. He stopped under it and took out a cigarette.

"You lookin' for someone, mate?" one of the stockmen on the bench asked.

"Not particularly," Oliver said.

He leaned against the trunk of the gum tree and watched the man raking another crop of grass to the smouldering fire.

There was something very peaceful, very calm about the place. It was old and shabby . . . yet it had an atmosphere. He wondered what it had been like when Carey had not been here. Echoing with loneliness and silence as Two Creeks had done when she left?

He'd never thought about love since he was a callow youth. He had never thought any one person, let alone a woman, could get under his skin.

He wasn't prepared to say what love was now. He knew that he wanted Carey . . . and he wasn't going home without her. He wanted her dear little face and her sweet, half-anxious smile. He wanted her young bright voice around the place at Two Creeks.

And he didn't want to make her afraid of him. Millicent had said he was an " academic judge." How does a judge of any kind get out of his robes, come down off his bench and woo the counsel pleading in the court?

Maybe he ought to behave just like any other man. . . .

A door behind him banged and Carey's voice came from the veranda.

" No, don't put the bin there, Danvers darling. Over there. . . . There by the tank-stand. . . ."

" Right-ee-o, Car—eee. How's that? She's right!"

" Bill! Bill!" It was Carey's pure clear voice. The man with the rake down at the fence stopped raking and turned.

" Me? You calling me, Car-ee?"

" Yes, I am, Bill."

Light feet ran down the steps . . . down the path. Towards the tree against which Oliver leaned . . . abreast of it.

Oliver put out his arm and caught Carey as she ran past. He swung her round, under the tree, and in another minute she was his his arms and he had kissed her hard on the lips.

154

Carey thrust herself backwards in the prison of his arms. The scarf round her head fell off.

"Oliver!" she said. "*You.*"

"Little deceiver," Oliver said, his voice coming roughly and strangely to his own ears. "So sweet and demure with those eyelashes resting on your cheeks and then looking up as if butter wouldn't melt in your mouth. . . . And all the time being the Shire President's off-sider for raising money . . . playing Pied Piper to the town children . . . winning bathing beauty competitions. Heaven knows what other sophistications. . . ."

"Oliver. Please. . . ."

There were heavy footsteps across the path and over Carey's shoulder Oliver could see a whole row of stockmen rolling ominously towards them.

"You must be a stranger round these parts, mister," said one. "Else you'd know you're likely to take a chip on the jaw from the whole gang, if you touch Car-ee."

Oliver did not release Carey.

"Well, chip away," he said. "She happens to be my wife and I'll kiss her how, when, where I like."

Oliver's voice had splinters of ice in it and he sounded as if he too could do a little of this chipping.

Carey twisted a little in Oliver's arms and turned her head towards the men.

"Darlings," she said gently. "You can go away. It's only my husband. And I love him. Though you mightn't think it by the way we act."

"You sure it's okay, Car-ee?"

She nodded.

"It's okay. I like it."

The men shuffled uneasily with their feet, then turned round and went back to the bench and the business of polishing harness.

Oliver shook Carey so that she turned her head back to him.

"You mean that, Carey?" he said.

"Yes, I mean it," she said. "But you don't have to hurt me, Oliver . . . and they are all looking at us. . . ."

"As if I care," he said. He crushed her to him and kissed her very soundly again. "Dear Heaven!" he said when he lifted his head. "Why didn't I do this before?"

"Yes, why didn't you?" said Carey.

"I don't know, my darling. I was crazy. I thought you were so young . . . so untouched by the tough things of life. Millicent said you were only a child. It was like . . . well, like forcing myself on someone so *young*. . . ."

"And Jane? What did Jane say?" Carey asked.

"Why should Jane say anything? What has Jane got to do with me and you?"

"She took you out on the veranda . . . at our wedding. And you were there so long. I was jealous, Oliver."

"You saw that, did you? My darling, I would give anything to have spared you that. Jane is just a too beautiful young woman who has got to have the admiration of every man she meets. If one appears to defect then her pride is hurt. She does something about it. But she's really only waiting for another conquest. She has to have them . . . like Alexander . . . one after another. When I was young and silly I wanted to beat the other lads to winning her. But that was only to show off."

Carey nodded her head soberly.

"I know now. She's out at Cartheroo station. Harry said as soon as she found out how wealthy those station owners were and what fun they have out there on the station she wouldn't have time to come into Wybong . . . even for you and me."

"Harry was right. As a matter of fact he's the rightest man I've ever met, Carey. Do you mind if I kiss you again, my sweet child?"

"On condition you don't call me a child."

"No, young woman. I promise. With all your experience of life . . . hospitals, children, bathing belles and the like . . . no one could call you an inexperienced child again. And darling, why didn't you tell me about Wybong? And your life here?"

Carey leaned back in Oliver's arms and laughed.

"Oh, Oliver, have you forgotten? You wouldn't let me tell you about Wybong." She sobered suddenly and then said very shyly, "I will tell you something, Oliver. I've never been kissed before."

"Never?"

"Not ever."

"Did I hurt you, dear?"

He put his hand up and touched her lips.

Carey leaned her head against his shoulder and slipped her arms under his arms and round him.

"It was wonderful," she said. She closed her eyes. It was still wonderful. It would go on being wonderful for ever.

She lifted her head.

"I think my stockmen have had quite enough of a free entertainment for one night, Oliver. We'd better go inside. And tell Uncle Tam."

They started to move away from under the shadow of the gum tree. Even in the approaching twilight they could see the white shine of the stockmen's teeth as they grinned.

"Millicent!" said Carey, suddenly stopping. "What will Millicent say . . . about our really loving one another? I mean . . ."

Oliver also stopped.

"Carey, tell me one thing more about Wybong. When a man asks a brother's permission to call on his sister, would he be courting?"

Carey gave a little cry of delight.

"Harry Martin would," she said. "He's dreadfully old-fashioned. His mother was like that. Everything had to be done just so, if you know what I mean. And Harry is always the same. Was it Harry? Oh, Oliver, wouldn't it be wonderful? Do you think Millicent *would*?"

"She wanted to come to Wybong very badly, and I felt all along it was something more than worrying about you . . . unless it was that you had run away with Harry Martin. Carey, do you tell the truth?"

"Absolutely always."

"Didn't you kiss Harry Martin in the railway yards when he first came to Preston?"

"Of course I did. Up here . . . like this. . . ."

Carey stood on tiptoe and putting her arms round Oliver kissed him on the brow.

"Very sweet, very nice," said Oliver as he raised his head and their eyes met. "But that's no kiss. Not like this." And he kissed her on the mouth again.

"Carey, do you come and stay with me at the hotel or do I come and stay with you at the Stockmen's Rest?"

Carey hesitated, then she said shyly:

"I suppose I had better answer as Ruth did in the Bible. Whither thou goest I will go. . . ."

"Then let's leave Jane to the millionaires and Millicent to Harry Martin's courting and go home to Two Creeks."

"Yes, Oliver. Please. I would love it so much. I miss

157

Tony . . . and Two Creeks "—then softly —" and you . . . so very much."

He turned her as if he would kiss her again but Carey put out a pleading hand.

"Those poor stockmen," she said.

"Poor devils," said Oliver. "Now it's their turn to be lonely."

He took her hand and they went towards the homestead in search of that wicked old schemer . . . Uncle Tam.

THE END

Novels of romance by

Lucy Walker

Love, misunderstanding, heartbreak, tenderness
. . . in the unfamiliar, exciting setting of Australia's vast Outback country.

THE OTHER GIRL. Three very different girls find themselves drawn to one man—and each is sure she'll lose him to one of the others.

HEAVEN IS HERE. Every girl within hundreds of miles was chasing Hugh Wilstack, and Jeannie vowed not to join the crowd. But her heart betrayed her. . . .

THE DISTANT HILLS. Angela was forced into a "marriage of convenience" through a cruel misunderstanding—could love grow from such a disastrous start?

SWEET AND FARAWAY. Lesley came out from England for her cousin's wedding—and found herself a virtual prisoner in the hands of the master of a vast Outback estate.

THE CALL OF THE PINES. Cherry came out to Yulinga as a governess, but a strange twist of fate threw her into a struggle for survival—and for the man she loved.

COME HOME, DEAR. Penny's love for John Dean had always seemed the most real thing in her life— then Ross Bennett came home. . . .

LOVE IN A CLOUD. Sonia loved John for his gentleness, Nick for his virile handsomeness—how could she decide?

FOLLOW YOUR STAR. Like many another girl, Kylie discovered the man she loved was an enigma— but she had to follow her star, wherever it might lead. . . .

HOME AT SUNDOWN. Two girls—and ten men— on a dangerous expedition, with feminine rivalry not the least of their perils.

REACHING FOR THE STARS. Ann came to Australia as an honored guest—and then found it had been a terrible mistake. . . .

A MAN CALLED MASTERS. It was Penny's chance for independence—but was she a match for the silent man who needed her?

THE STRANGER FROM THE NORTH. She had to do a man's job—and was doing it well . . . until the stranger rode in and took over.

THE RIVER IS DOWN. She had crossed her own Rubicon—now she was free to be a different woman, with a new life.

THE ONE WHO KISSES. Had Hal changed, or had he always been selfish and cruel? And how did he measure up to someone like Rick?

THE MAN FROM OUTBACK. Mari was whisked off to Australia to mend a broken heart—but as soon as she met Kane Manners, her heart was in trouble again. . . .

DOWN IN THE FOREST. The tragedy of the fire had reached them all—but, in its embers, Jill sensed that her dreams might come true.

WIFE TO ORDER. Her guardian had treated Carey as a child—and now he told her coldly that she would soon be his wife. . . .

THE MOONSHINER. Joan fled the social whirl for life in the vast Outback. She learned much of the ways of the wild—and then she learned to love. . . .

THE RANGER IN THE HILLS. Was he a myth or a man? Now that he held her in his arms, Kate would discover the truth about the man she had had to trust.

To order by mail, send 80¢ for each book to Dept. CS, Beagle Books, 36 West 20 Street, New York, NY 10011.